Forsaken

Gerard Lee

NEW ISLAND

FORSAKEN
First published 2014
by New Island
16 Priory Office Park
Stillorgan
County Dublin
www.newisland.ie

Copyright © Gerard Lee, 2014
Gerard Lee has asserted his moral rights.

PRINT ISBN: 978-1-84840-361-1
EPUB ISBN: 978-1-84840-362-8
MOBI ISBN: 978-1-84840-363-5

British Library Cataloguing Data. A CIP catalogue record for this book is available from the British Library

Typeset by JVR Creative India
Cover design by New Island
Printed by ScandBook AB Sweden

New Island received financial assistance from
The Arts Council (An Comhairle Ealaíon), Dublin, Ireland

10 9 8 7 6 5 4 3 2 1

For Paula, Mollyrose and Nancy

When I was five the black dreams came;
Nothing after was quite the same.
Come back early or never come.

Louis MacNeice, 'Autobiography'

His heart was filled with broken wings
And rag-flowers, feeble worthless things.

Federico Garcia Lorca, 'Suicide'
(Trans: Merryn Williams)

ONE

WHEN I WAS TEN, MY FATHER went up a tree and never came down. For a long time nobody knew where he was, though they searched and searched everywhere. They even looked in the lake, where him and me used to catch prickly perch and slimy black eels. Imagine looking in the lake! I could have told them, if anyone had bothered to ask me, that nobody would hide in the lake, least of all my da, and definitely not in the middle of the cold winter when you could skim flat stones across the ice near the shore. There wasn't even a boat to hide in, because they were all taken up for the winter to get cleaned and fixed up and painted. The only boat left out was a half-sunk one that you couldn't properly hide in, unless you were a mallard duck, or a sly pike.

Mammy said that I went round and round the house and down the lane calling, 'Come out, come out, wherever you are. We all give up,' for weeks after Da vanished, but that's not true. It was really for a few months that I did it, but only when Mam wasn't around, because she said it was upsetting her. I did it in a whisper, the way the old people say their confessions to Father Nealon. If you were next in line for the confession box, you could always hear the first part: 'Bless me, Father, for I have sinned.' Then the sinners must have remembered that the people waiting next in the pew, the ones pretending to pray, but who were all ears really, would love to hear their neighbours' bad sins, and race off up the town to tell everyone. So the rest of the confessions always got very whispery. That was the way I called to Da in the lane. If anyone had heard me, they would have thought the priest was hearing confessions under the hedge, like they had to do when the English were here. I didn't know then that searching for Da was going to turn into the longest game of hide-and-seek ever. Eventually we all gave up trying to find him. Even I hadn't got the faintest idea where he was. I started to leave little notes in the lane and in the barn to say to him that he had the game well won, but it was still over a year before Da gave us so much as a clue.

Da did his big vanishing trick at Hallowe'en. Mammy didn't say much for the first few days, because he always came back eventually. Then, after a few days went by with still no sign of him, Mam started to fret over him like an old clucking hen, and she told everyone in the parish to keep a good eye out for him. That's when the searching really started. I bet Da would have loved that, watching the whole town running around like a crowd of headless chucks, all on his account. That's when they looked in the lake. I was dying to tell him about that part, because he'd have burst his shirt laughing at that carry-on. Burst sideways like a sheep in clover so he would. Mammy took awful bad with the worry, but I was going around with a big smile most of the time, because I knew my da had just outfoxed the lot of them.

'One of these mornings we'll be down for the breakfast, and Da will be there at the kitchen table ahead of us all, grinning like the cat that got the cream,' I said to Mammy.

But nothing I could say would cheer her up. The search went on for weeks, and I kept calling Da to just come out for the love of God, and let them all see. But he never showed.

They searched on and off all November, depending on the weather. It teemed rain for a fortnight, then Jack Frost went on the skite for another fortnight. Even the robin was gone from Mammy's wee garden. Then in December, after years of waiting for a white Christmas, it snowed like billy-o. It snowed for three whole days. It was the most snow I'd ever seen in my life. On the second day my mammy and me made a huge snowman, nearly as tall as she was.

'Maybe we could bring our snowman into the house and pretend he's Da,' I said, when it was time to go in. 'Then Da will see in at the window that there's a stranger in the house, and he'll come crashing through the trees and burst in through the door like Tarzan to rescue us.'

I could sort of do the Tarzan noise a bit. I did it for Mam, beating my fists on my chest. She laughed, just one big sudden burst of a laugh. She hadn't really laughed properly for ages, not since Hallowe'en, when Da put his big overcoat on backwards and got a colander that fitted on top of his head. He came after me in the kitchen with his arms out straight like Frankenstein in one of the Hammer horror films he liked to watch.

'Fee Fi Fo Fum, I smell the blood of an Englishman. Be he alive or be he dead, I'll grind his bones to make my bread.'

After a while I went out looking for apples and monkey nuts at the neighbours' houses, and by the time I got back, Da was gone off hiding.

I was glad to see the snow, not just because there was finally enough to make a proper snowman, but because I thought I could use it like a hunter, to finally track Da down.

'We could even put a saucepan on the snowman's head,' I said to Mam, 'and he'd definitely be like Da.'

After that, she started to cry again, and say Da's name over and over like in a prayer. Then she didn't move or say anything for a long time. She was sitting beside me all the time with her arm around me, both of us shivering. Usually Mammy would have me wrapped up in so many coats that I could hardly move my arms, so sitting beside her in the cold like that was sort of a strange carry-on, but I liked it and didn't want to spoil it by complaining about the cold. It was getting dark, and more snow was blowing around and piling up. Mam looked at me for a long time without noticing that my teeth were chattering. Then she said that she thought the snowman was really more like her than Da.

'Well, I know he's as tall as you, and he has your good hat and scarf on, but Mammy, even if we called him a snowlady instead of a snowman, you still don't look one bit like him.'

She smiled and said what she'd meant was that the snowman would not be there for ever. I didn't know what she was talking about, and I didn't care, because it was just good to see her smiling a bit again and talking, and us having good fun, and I didn't want to spoil it by asking stupid questions. I was sure Da would be back for Christmas.

From as far back as I can remember, hiding was his favourite game. Sometimes it was just for the day, and a night maybe. Other times I didn't see him for a few days, and then I'd ask Mammy if she knew where he was.

'He must be hiding someplace,' was all she'd say.

Well I knew that farm of ours backways, frontways and inside out, even in the dark, and still I was hardly ever able to catch him. Between you and me, though, he cheated. Often I'd stay awake late when I was seven or eight, watching from my window, to see if I could catch him sneaking out from of his hideout, and sometimes I'd see him coming along the lane from the road. The road! That was way out of bounds, and everyone knew that.

One time I even asked my mother if she knew where he was hiding, and she said probably in the town. In the town! Total cheating. I remember another time when I was still small, six I think because I got my Chopper bike then; I came into the kitchen to check if he was in there, and she was on her own, crying. I asked her if it was because Da was too good at hiding and she said, sort of, that it was. Sure, how could she be expected to look for him in the town, help me do my homework, and put the dinner on and all the rest of it? I think that's why she never really found the time to have another baby, after me.

No matter where he was, he must have been afraid to go out to the toilet in case he'd be caught, because he was always bursting to go when he'd get home. That'd be the first big thing you'd hear when he got in at night, and when he'd think it was safe to come out from hiding. If you left the aluminium bucket for making up the calves' feed under the high tap in the yard, and the tap full on, that was like the noise. Not just once in the night, a few times maybe. Who knows how many, because I was probably asleep for half of them.

He must have kept Mammy awake too, because she was often very tired-looking in the morning. She'd be real cross with me about a lost sock or a school-book, or not finishing my porridge or something. Then after a while she'd say she was sorry. I wanted to tell her that it was alright, but I was too embarrassed to say that I knew it was Daddy's business in the toilet that was keeping her awake, that he was just taking the games of hide-and-seek too far, and that he was too late coming home. And then, in the toilet, sounding like our neighbour Con Grealish playing his trumpet after too much porter.

Da banged doors open and shut again, very hard, and sometimes he'd be talking loud, like somebody was with him. Or arguing even. I'd look through the crack in my door, though, and he was always on his own. Maybe he was sleep-arguing.

Then the other noises from the jacks, like a cow stuck down a well, wanting to get out. Or a dog barking backwards. Then the tap going off and on in the metal calves bucket, followed by one more groan from the trapped cow, and a flush at last.

The Christmas before Da did his biggest ever hide-and-seek, I got a new digital watch from Santy, and sometimes I used to time my da in the toilet. Once he took two minutes and forty-eight seconds! How could a person have so much widdle? Maybe if you were hiding all day and didn't widdle once, maybe then, but he was already after going a while earlier – I'd heard him. I think he went in the ditch or in the lane too, most nights.

All Mam would ever say was, 'If you put a lot of something in, then a lot has to come out.' I'd just agree, though I didn't know what she was talking about. I often did that then, just agreed with her, because sometimes she didn't seem to like all my questions. I think I was a bit of a nuisance sometimes in those days, though Mammy would never say that. She would never want to hurt anybody's feelings, not even people who hurt hers. In town everyone said Mam was a quiet and kind poor soul, and that she would do anything for anybody, and that it was all a terrible shame, a terrible shame.

What was a terrible shame, I wanted to know? Nobody would tell me. 'The weather, JJ,' was all she'd say, if I asked.

The neighbours all started to carry on as if they were in the confession box every time Mammy and me passed them by.

So I gave up asking. The weather wasn't all that bad, so either my mother didn't know herself what the terrible shame was, or she was telling a fib, and I didn't believe my mother would ever tell a fib. She said that when a person told her a lie, it offended her and it offended God, and my mother was always praying to God, so why would she want to offend Him? She would never curse or shout, or do anything bad either. Even if my da cursed, which he often did. Or if he shouted, or was rude some other way. Like he'd let wind in the kitchen, loud and on purpose, in a way that nobody could ignore. Even if you could ignore the loudness of it, the whiff was like someone had lifted the cover off the slurry pit on a hot summer's day, so Mammy would just have to say something.

'Did someone blow?' she'd say.

Then he'd say, 'No, chicken,' because he often called her that, 'but somebody definitely cracked an ojeously horrid fart. Was that you, JJ? You dirty article! Next time would you at least pop your arse out over the half-door.'

She'd go all red then and start peeling potatoes, no matter what time of the day it was. I thought it was sort of funny, no matter how often I'd heard it, but I didn't laugh because I knew Mammy didn't really like it. I'd even go outside if I had to laugh, or – worse – if I really had to do one myself, so Mam wouldn't hear it and be even more embarrassed.

'It's all right, son,' Da said. 'Didn't God Himself say: "Wherever ye be, let your wind blow free, in church or chapel let it rattle"? Oh aye, I believe it was indeed God Himself who said that. He said it to the disciples, in the Book of Flutheronomy, I think it was.'

Mammy didn't like it when Da started jeering about God, so then I usually just put on my wellies and got the calves s bucket or the hens' scraps, and went out to the yard.

Sometimes in those days, long before Da did his last big vanishing act, I'd come in from school or from fishing, or from bringing hay up to the fields, days when Da wasn't anywhere to be found, and she would be sitting there, just staring. Staring at the range or the radio or the floor. The first few times I saw her that way, I remember thinking something terrible was after happening, and that she just didn't know how to tell me yet.

'The hamster got out and Neelo ate him,' maybe.

Except Neelo, our old dog, went under Brady's Cortina when I was five and a half. He was chasing a scrawny class of a chicken of Phil Reilly's across the road at the time. Neelo was buried afterwards in Mammy's little garden at the side of the house. Of course Reilly's chicken made the far ditch, but Da belted it with the spade the next time it strayed into our yard looking for a free dinner. So maybe not that exactly, but something bad like that anyway was on Mammy's mind.

Next thing she'd see me standing there and sit up and say she never heard me coming in. If I asked her was something bad after happening, she'd say not at all. 'I was just trying to think of what to have for the dinner, is all.'

That was a relief, because I also was a bit afraid that Mammy might be after finding my wet sheets and pyjamas stuck in the press where I'd leave them every morning till I'd get in from school, and be cross. But the sheets were always gone and fresh ones on the bed. And clean pyjamas too. Every time I thought I was getting out of my bed-wetting at last, it stopped and then started again. I wanted to explain that that was all Da's fault too, that I couldn't go to the toilet with him in there sleep-arguing and pushing cows down the well. But I was afraid that if Mammy gave out to him he might go and hide in an even harder place than before, a new hideout that nobody would ever find, and that would make Mammy even more sad and cross. So I never said. Mammy never mentioned it either, except when it was raining a lot, and then she'd say it was hard to get all the clothes dry, especially the sheets, and she'd sort of look at me.

'Well, what are we having for dinner so, Mam?' I'd ask.

'Ants' kneecaps and spiders' toenails,' she'd say, and we'd start laughing, and forget about staring at nothing, and worrying about pongy sheets.

Even though I never said anything to get him in trouble, Da still went off and hid in an awful hard place in the end.

TWO

MAMMY WAS ALWAYS VERY HOLY, even in the times before my da started hiding. But during the weeks after he decided to get into the *Guinness Book of Records* as the World's Greatest Hider, Mam became a fair world-class prayer, too. She prayed and prayed and prayed and prayed and prayed and prayed and prayed and prayed and prayed. Does that sound like a lot? You should have been in our house then, because if you were you'd say, 'Let you add a few more "prayeds" to that list.' She prayed so much, I was afraid she would forget how to unpray, if there's such a thing. Or how to be not praying, maybe.

There were masses, novenas, vigils, rosaries and other things I can't even remember the names of. Vigils were the worst. All the mothers in the place gathered in one corner of the church, with me sometimes stuck in the middle of them, all staring, like Mammy was always doing, at the sad statues. I wondered if Mammy wished she could be a statue. Sometimes it was hard to tell the difference between all the holy mammies, and the actual statues. I thought if Mam wasn't careful, God might want to bring her up to Heaven early, so she could show all the angels and saints what real praying was.

She had this trick too, if you interrupted her in the middle of a Hail Mary, where she would say, 'Just give me one minute,' without losing where she was in the prayer, and then carry on to the end of it. Then, eventually, she'd quietly fold away all her little holy leaflets with special prayers to all sorts of saints, with pictures of roses and little children, like me, listening to whatever the saints were saying. Then she'd put her rosary beads into a little brown leather purse with a gold clasp.

'God will help us to save your poor daddy, but we must pray very hard for God to hear us.'

'I suppose so,' I said, and left it at that. I didn't know what she was talking about with her 'save your poor daddy'. He was just too good at hiding, but there was no point in talking.

By December Mam must have decided that God was not doing enough looking, because she finally agreed to go on the television news, to see if that would help us to find him, and to say to Da, if he happened to be watching, to please come home for Christmas. I thought he'd be over the moon to be on the news himself, since he never missed it. Mam got all done up like she was off to a wedding. She took down this big blue hat from the top of their wardrobe, and stuck it on with a needle with a red plastic ball on the end of it. She insisted on wearing the hat in the house. She put on a matching blue dress. The dress looked like an accordion that someone had wrapped around her tummy. Then she put on her Sunday Mass coat with the big buttons. She said she would do an interview only in her own house, not above in any studio.

'Mammy, you look like someone off the television,' I said.

'JJ, I'm going to do this so your father will see that we really love him and want him back. Please, JJ, don't upset me now.'

'I just don't see how that big hat is going to convince Da,' I said and she shot me a look that would turn a funeral up a side street, so I kept my trap shut after that.

I wiped down the kitchen table and tidied around a bit, while she practised with her bachelor brother, my Uncle Patsy, what she was going to say when the camera crowd would arrive. I still didn't see how a big hat was going to convince my da of anything, but I didn't want to upset her, so I said no more about it. But that wasn't the worst of it. No sooner was the camera on Mammy than she started crying.

'Tom, oooh, Tom love, we all love you and we miss you terrible bad. I can't go much longer without you. Come home ... please ... come home to us ... ooh, Tom.'

Before they could start persuading Mammy to drag me on to the couch with her for the camera, I slipped off to my own hideout in the barn. I got hungry later on, though, and a bit scared when Mammy went back in and stopped looking and calling for me. By then I had at least five minutes of wee that I badly needed to do. And it was still freezing, even though the snow was all well gone.

I tried to imagine what would happen if I stayed hiding too long and couldn't hold it in any more.

'Mam?'

' ... the Lord is with thee ... just give me one minute ... blessed art thou amongst women, and blessed is the fruit of thy womb, Jesus. Yes, JJ, what is it?'

'I'm afraid I've a bit of bad news, Mam.'

'What, JJ, what's happened? Is it about your father?'

'No, Mam. It's more serious than that. I've wet the barn. All the hay is sopping, really wringing wet. On top of that, I melted the last of the snow, and that wet it more.'

'Holy Mary, Mother of God, pray for us sinners.'

Bad enough doing it in the bed, but the poor cows might have starved on account of me, so I went back in before it was too late. I was always careful, though, not to give away my hideout, and so I did what rabbits do. Rabbits are very clever. I read a great book that was just new in school, *Watership Down,* and it was all about rabbits. They always have an emergency escape burrow, or more than one, somewhere far away from the main hole. If a fox or a badger or a dog, or even a farmer tries to trap them, the crafty little rabbit just nips out a back way, and leaves them all digging and shouting, 'We nearly have him', when they nearly have no such thing. So when I finally decided it was safe to go back in, I left my hideout by the emergency exit, just to be sure.

It was pitch dark when I came in, and Mammy was on the phone. She was crying again. Then she heard me shivering or coughing behind her. I think she was calling the gardaí to get the sniffer dogs out to look for me. She should have just asked our neighbour Phil Reilly to send his dog Spinner. Spinner always knew how to find me. Me and Spinner were the best of pals, and he would have known where to look. He'd have found me straight away.

You'd think when Da was off hiding, at least Mammy would have had some sleep. No more doors banging. No more waterfalls in the middle of the night, or trapped cows. The thing is, she never slept at all then. The day wasn't long enough for all the praying and staring she wanted to do, and sometimes she had to get up in the middle of the night and do a bit more. I mustn't have been getting any better sleep either, because sometimes I'd come downstairs in my pyjamas, and there she'd be, having a staring match with the range.

'Can you not get to sleep?' I'd ask her, but she didn't want to lose the staring match by looking away first, so she

13

wouldn't answer me for ages, or not while I was still there in the kitchen. Once or twice while I was going slowly back up the stairs, I heard her saying in a whisper, *Jesus,* or *JJ,*or something like that. Other times I must have been asleep again before she said anything, because I mostly didn't hear any answer. She was trying to figure out where Da was hiding, and win the staring match, and decide what to have for dinner, and probably think what to get me for Christmas. Is it any wonder she had no mind left for silly questions? The only thing was: no matter how long she spent thinking about dinner in those days, she still could never decide, and we often ended up having no dinner at all. We'd have a rosary instead, and a couple of novenas for dessert.

School days before the Christmas holidays were grand, because you could get food in the big break. You were supposed to pay for it, but we never had any money. Mrs Logan in the school kitchen didn't seem to mind, though, and she always gave me loads of everything. I'd tell her to write it all down, and that my da would settle up with her. Then she'd just have a look on her face like she was a sad statue in the chapel too. I think she was another one who did a lot of practice with novenas and vigils.

At weekends I mostly ate porridge, bread and cheese. Mam didn't seem to be hungry at all. Neighbours said she would need to start taking proper care of herself or she would fade away to nothing. I thought that was stupid. How could a person just fade away to nothing?

Mind you, over the next while, Mammy did sort of get smaller. There was definitely less of her than there used to be.

It was a strange time for old JJ, all right: a vanished Da, and a melting Mammy.

THREE

PRAYING. NOTHING MUCH ELSE happened in my house for a long time. The television lads went off to where someone else was crying even louder than Mammy. Da mustn't have seen the news the day Mam was on, bawling in her big blue hat, because he still didn't appear. Or else he didn't recognise her under the hat, or if he did he was too embarrassed to admit that he knew her. I wouldn't have blamed him. God mustn't have seen the news either, because we had to spend our first Christmas ever without my da.

That wasn't really a Christmas at all. We looked at the Pope saying Mass on the television, and then we visited the cemetery to put flowers on my grandparents' graves. They'd all been dead for years, but Mammy still cried when she went to the graveyard. She said her mother held me in her arms for five minutes before she died, just after I was born. Mam told me that every time we went to the cemetery, and then she started crying.

The best present, apart from my da coming home, would have been if Mammy had stopped crying for Christmas. A lot of people gave my mother statues and pictures of Jesus on the cross, and Jesus dead in His mother's arms, which probably reminded her of little me in her mother's arms, and gave her prayers about how much better things would get when we were all dead. I know about the prayers, because Mammy used to make me read them if I ever said I was bored. I didn't really know what was the point of us all being born in the first place if all we were going to do was spend our whole life looking forward to being dead.

Anyway, I stopped telling Mammy I was bored fairly soon after being made to read a few of those prayers. The house was still full of statues and big pictures of Jesus being crucified, or being scourged with thorns, or lying dead in His mother's arms. Mam put them up all around the house. There was a big one in my bedroom and it gave me nightmares, but she wouldn't let me take it down. Jesus looked like He'd got a belt from the creamery truck, crossing the road. And Da still didn't show.

I played a lot with Phil Reilly's dog Spinner during my Christmas holidays from school, when Uncle Patsy wasn't making me work the farm. Me and Spinner sometimes had a sneaky look for Da too, but I never said that to Mammy. Uncle Patsy usually had me doing work on his farm as well as our own, and I often wished the holidays were over and I was back in school. He used to send me home at dinnertime, even when I was after working all day on his farm, and he hadn't a good word to throw to a dog. I started to really detest my Uncle Patsy. I got sick to the pit of my stomach of some people since then, but I hated Uncle Patsy more than I ever hated anybody. He made a woeful bad Christmas worse.

We didn't really have any decorations to take down on the sixth of January, just the crib, which was all Mammy wanted to put up that year. It was very quiet most of the time around our house. There was no Da making noise, and not many people called either. I think our house would have made them all feel too depressed. Father Nealon sometimes came by for a visit, and often Dr Cassidy would be with him. When any of them came around, or if I saw Uncle Patsy walking across the field from his house, I'd just go out the back door as quietly as I could and look for Spinner. I pretended I was all holy to Father Nealon if I met him, so he would think I was as religious as Mammy. I think even the priest was a bit scared of a few of my mother's statues of Jesus being whipped and tortured, though he would never say that. I saw him looking a bit funny at them a few times. Once he saw me looking at him, and I sort of threw my eyes up to Heaven, just to let him know that I understood what he meant, but he looked very puzzled at me, so I never let on again. He was probably afraid he would end up in trouble with Mammy or the Pope or someone.

I was glad to get back to school after that no-good Christmas, and to Mrs Logan's school dinners. Uncle Patsy couldn't really get me to do much work then either, because it was dark when I'd get home. The weather was too bad for doing much work on the farm, because it was bitter cold and sleeting all the time.

Mammy loved nature, and she liked to list off all the flowers that came as a sign of spring.

'Snowdrops first, then crocuses, then daffodils. And the cherry tree – there comes a lovely blossom on that in the spring.'

She said other ones, but the names were in a foreign language. I loved the snowdrops too, because my birthday was soon after them. Crows and magpies started fixing up their old battered nests from the previous year, even before the big sticky buds were open. Mammy didn't once go out to her little garden, but things still started to grow in it anyway. Not all neat and tidy the way Mam liked to have her plants usually, but wild, sort of, and any old which way. Like an old willow tree Da showed me once down near the River Weal. The tree was all twisted, like an old man with a broken, crooked back. Da told me that a cow coming down to the river for a drink had stood on the little seedling years before and damaged it, but didn't quite fully break it, and that was why the tree grew all bent and rickety and wrong-ways. Well, that's what Mammy's little garden was like – everything kept growing, but it was all gone a bit wonky.

Spinner started to bury bones in Mammy's old garden, because the ground was soft and easy to dig. Mammy had raked over it so many times, there wasn't even a stone left in it, and now that she didn't want to be bothered any more, Spinner decided he might as well have it for hiding bones in. He dug up some flower bulbs, with the little green shoots just starting to come up. That would usually have driven Mam half-cracked, but she didn't even notice. Or if she did, she just didn't care. After a few visits from Spinner, Mammy's flower garden looked more like a bone garden. That's what Da called the graveyard – the bone garden. Maybe Spinner thought that if you planted bones, they'd grow, that you'd come out some day and find a crop of ripe skeletons swaying in the breeze.

That's all I really remember until my eleventh birthday came around, on the twenty-second of February. Da didn't appear at the kitchen table to sing 'Happy Birthday', Mammy didn't get finished with her praying, and Uncle Patsy kept trying to get me out to work on his farm. Mam was so busy at her prayers, she forgot to buy me a birthday present. I wrote it down on a piece of paper to give Da: 'You owe JJ a present for last Christmas. And another one for his eleventh birthday.'

Then Uncle Patsy said to Mammy that we'd have to sell some calves or a few sheep.

'You've no one to tend them, and I can't do it all. Sell, and get shut of the worry. You'll have a few shillings in the house itself then.'

He said that as a favour to us he'd buy them, and give us a fair price. 'I've more bastes than I can manage, but if it would help you out now, I'll do it in the name of God.'

I didn't trust Uncle Patsy, though, and I asked a few men when I was getting messages for Mammy in town what price calves would fetch in the market. I told her what they said.

'Uncle Patsy isn't giving us half of what the calves are worth, the men told me.'

But she didn't care.

'Poor Uncle Patsy is doing us a good turn, bringing the animals into the mart for us, and he's been working hard on our land too,' she said. 'It's only fair if he makes a few shillings on it.'

'Poor Uncle Patsy? He's robbing us blind, robbing his own sister.' Mammy was praying again, and she didn't listen.

Uncle Patsy had a long face that could kiss a goat between the horns. Spinner did more work on our farm than Uncle Patsy ever did. I wished my da would come out and give him a belt of the spade. What did we need money for anyway? Unless maybe Mrs Logan in the school kitchen wanted to be paid for all the dinners. The neighbour men who came by to help would ask me how my mother was, and I'd tell them she was grand, and doing fierce praying altogether.

'And by the way, men,' I said, 'if you're thinking of shifting any cows or sheep, my Uncle Patsy will take them off your hands. He'll even bring them into the mart and sell them, and he won't charge you a penny – or give you a penny either.'

They'd all laugh a bit, and then stop and look at each other, and nod and say, 'That's good, that's good,' and then go flopping off up the fields in their big cow-shit wellies and their arses half-out of their trousers, and their big sweaty necks swarming with horseflies and bluebottles and midges, and they carrying bales of hay and wire to fix fences. They all wore caps that looked the same, with nothing under them but soft wrinkly skin.

Then their wives would go into our house and sit with Mammy, and cook and bake a bit, and do some praying too, of course. Sometimes I'd come in when they'd be just getting up off their knees after a few dozen rosaries, and they'd be saying silly things in front of Mammy.

'Maybe 'tis all for the best.'

'Sure 'twould never come right anyhow.'

Rubbish like that. I wouldn't even ask them what it was supposed to mean, because I knew they would answer with something even more ridiculous, the kind of stupid answer I used to get to the 'terrible shame' question. The baking was good, though, and luckily my mother didn't take one blind bit of notice of what the silly women said. She just kept on asking God to find Da, or save him. I didn't even argue about what way she said it any more. If God was half as good as the people around here were always saying He was, He'd have known what was needed, and He'd have done something about it a long time before that. But He didn't. How many times did you have to ask?

Nobody knew where my da was; God didn't know, the gardaí didn't know, my mother didn't know, the television boys didn't know, even Spinner, the dog that Da said could have found Little Bo Peep's sheep, even he didn't know.

So we sold any calves we had, and a few lambs, and then the dozen milk cows that Da hadn't sold already, to

Uncle Patsy. When it came to buying them, Uncle Patsy had another story for my mother and me.

'The mart is gone very bad these few weeks. I might have to hold on to them for a while, till I see if I can get a price for them. But I'll not leave you stuck. Here's a few bob to be getting along with.'

What he gave my mam wouldn't buy feed for a bantam hen, and I knew he had no intention of giving her a penny more either. Mammy was just too nice. On top of that she was too sad, and too busy praying to notice, or care. She gave most of the money to the priest to say a load of Masses and novenas and vigils to find Da. Maybe she couldn't afford the really dear Masses and novenas, the very best ones. Or maybe she just couldn't pay for enough of them. Whatever it was, Da still never appeared. Mammy belted me and sent me to my bedroom to say an act of contrition when I asked her why the priest couldn't say the Masses on tick till Da was back making us some money again.

'After all, my presents are all down on tick, and Mrs Logan has all my dinners on tick too.'

'That's Satan talking,' she said.

'Well, if that's Satan's idea, then he's a deal smarter than folks around these parts generally give him credit for.'

Mam went for the wooden spoon then, but I was in my room before the drawer stopped rattling.

The weather slowly started to get nicer, and everything in the country was growing like mad. The animals started to get frisky, feeling the sun on their backs again. When we had loads of sheep and they were all having lambs, the lambs jumped around like they were drunk men at a ceili dance. You'd get up in the morning, and lambs would be after sprouting up in the fields during the night like mushrooms.

Now our sheep were all gone to the mart, or else they were over having their lambs on Uncle Patsy's farm. Our fields were very quiet that year – there wasn't even a cowpat for the poor crows to peck. They just stood around the fields with their hands crossed behind their backs, like the men coming from Mass. Still, the rabbits were nearly just as frisky as the lambs used to be. A few little whiskery noses bobbed out of their burrows, when the first of the new spring babies dared each other to see who'd go outside first.

One night about a month or so before I got my summer holidays, I heard something in the yard that made me jump out of bed like a shot. First I was sure it was Da. But when I ran to the window, there was Mammy crossing the gate to the big hill field, in her nightdress. I looked to see was Da calling her, or where she was going at that hour in her nightdress.

She looked as if she was in a sort of trance, the way she was walking. There was no sign of Da that I could make out, so I ran downstairs and out after her. I called to her a few times, but she didn't seem to hear me. She kept walking and stumbling across the field, up towards where the old Fairy Fort was. I thought maybe the fairies were calling her. Then I wondered if they had my da too, and now here they were, coming for the rest of the family – that would explain everything. They could take a person like that if they wanted to, Mammy often said so herself. Then they'd put a stick in the bed where the person was, and the stick would swell up and grow and take the exact shape of that person, and by the time the real people figured out what had happened, it would be too late. All you'd be left with was the old stick-person, cackling away at you with a laugh like an old man's death rattle.

If it was the fairies, I knew I'd have to bring her back before she went through their secret door in the roots of the big oak tree in the middle of the Fairy Fort. She often showed me that big oak tree when we'd be out in the fields checking animals, or moving them to another field, or bringing them hay. Or just when we would be out walking, like we often used to do, each of us secretly half-looking for Da but not telling the other we were doing it. Even if we got caught in a big shower of rain, Mammy would never shelter under that old tree, or even so much as sit on the wall of the fort. Well, they would have to take me and my mother together now, I decided, because I sure wasn't going to stay in our house on my own if the fairies took her away too. It wouldn't be too bad, under the oak tree, as long as we were all together again – Mam, Da and me.

It was pitch dark, but I could see her nightdress kind of glowing in the middle of a field, like a ghost, or a sheep, or a snow-woman. When I caught up with her, the fairy spell must have made her think that I was Da, because she started to say she had the tea ready and to hurry now or it would be cold.

It was the fairies right enough – I knew then straight away – because they had her talking through her hat. I turned her around slowly and led her back into the house. Her face was strange, like she was already halfway gone over to them. I think I got her just in time. I'd say the fairies were raging, because they don't like anyone to cross them, but as far as I was concerned, they could take someone else's mother.

It could be that they swore that night to get their revenge on me, because Mammy always said that fairies are very spiteful. There was no stick in her bed when we got back, and Mam just got in quietly and went off to sleep. I never said anything about it in the morning, and Mam couldn't remember anyhow, probably from the spell they had on her. At least nobody saw the pair of us that time, out in the middle of a field in the heel of the night, in our pyjamas, and we talking about the tea getting cold.

Then she started going off out every few nights, calling Da in the darkness. I didn't really mind too much. I kind of liked being out with her again, even if it was the night-time. At least the nosey neighbours couldn't see us, and it was getting into summer then, and the weather wasn't as bad. I just followed her in one of Da's old coats. Then I'd talk to her, in a kind of a man's voice, like I'd often heard Da.

'I was delayed in the town on some business, so I was, and I've had the tea and all that. Now, girl, we should get off to the bed, because it's late, and tomorrow'll be on us before we know it.'

That usually got her back to the house and into her bed without any fuss. Once the summer holidays started, though, the fairies must have got very determined to have their way. Neighbours started calling in all the time, a few times a day, saying they only wanted what was best for my mother and me. It began to really annoy me after a while, like I couldn't be trusted to take care of my own mother, especially when I wasn't getting proper sleep, following her across the fields three or four nights every week, and trying to make sure nobody saw us either.

'We only want to help, JJ,' they'd say.

They'd even have rosary beads, to make themselves look all holy.

'Grand. Help us look for my da so,' I said to them. 'He's around here somewhere.'

'But ... '

That's all you'd ever get from them then.

'But.'

Mam prayed through it all.

'... to thee do we fly, poor banished children of Eve', was all she had to say.

Then the women would all whisper a bit, take out their rosary beads, and join in with my mother. At least they'd stop talking for a while about what was best for us all. Other people came too, trying to get my mother to go someplace with them for *a rest*.

They must have thought I came down in the last shower. They said they were people. You see, that's how sly fairies can be. Because they could make themselves look like friendly neighbours, or doctors, or anyone you like. Probably even God if they wanted to, saying they were only trying to help you. Maybe some of them were real neighbours too, but I knew then that I'd have to be careful who was who, and which ones I trusted.

'Hello, JJ. You don't know me, but my name is God. I'd like to bring your mother out for a wee walk in the field, and a chat about a few private matters, and see how everything is going for her, if that's alright?'

'You're no more God than that crowing cock above on the wall. Now get on out of it, or I'll fix you with a barrel of my da's shotgun.'

That's just one way they had of trying to get into the house. Then when they'd be in, they'd grab you, and leave a stick to cod everyone. But me and my mother were too cute to be taken in by their tricks and their sticks. As the summer went on, I knew I had to stop them from getting in, so they couldn't take Mammy off for this famous rest, or for anything else that she didn't need. A daddy back home where he belonged was all she needed, and all I needed too. Simple. If they all thought they knew what was best for us, how come none of them were able to come up with that simple answer? I was only eleven, and even I knew that much. But as usual they were all far too busy telling us what they thought we needed to be bothered listening to, instead of what we might actually think ourselves. Whispering and nodding to each other as if I hadn't a clue what they were up to.

I realised then that I'd have to make sure they didn't lure Mammy outside any more. It was just lucky for me they never got to her on one of her midnight walks. I was too quick for them. Still, I knew there was no way I could take any chances. Once the fairies or the shee or the pucas or the will-o'-the-wisps or the little folk or whatever the hell they were started to realise that I was up to all their tricks, they would try something new, something nasty, something I wasn't prepared for.

I knew they would try to separate us. They did it with my da, but they'd never fool me again. I had outsmarted them that first night in the field, and many times since, and now they realised they had a sharp little boyo to get past before they could steal my mother away. It was pretty clear by then that they didn't want to be bothered taking me too. I was probably too smart for their world; I'd only cause trouble for them, trying to escape and telling all the other human prisoners their antics. I'd be like that Darby O'Gill who tricked the Fairy King.

So I decided to tell the neighbour women that we didn't want any more buns or scones or cakes or stews or hairy bacon.

'We're giving up cake anyway, me and Mammy,' I said, 'and sure I can help her cook the dinner now. We don't need any more help with the rosary either. My mother knows it off by heart, as you may have noticed, and she can do it on her own just grand, thanks. Or she can give it out and I can answer it. So you needn't trouble yourselves coming round at all. You have enough else to pray for. Be good statues now and go on back to the chapel, or under the oak tree, and bring your fiddlesticks and your beads with you. Fly, poor banished children of Eve.'

'But.'

Oh yes, but.

Plenty of buts, in fact.

'But nothing,' I said, as cool as you like.

More whispering and nodding. I nearly laughed to see them – they hadn't a clue what to say to all that. Only 'but'.

'But what about the rest of the animals?' they said eventually.

I knew they wouldn't give up easily, but I had figured out how to fox them.

'We're going to keep one cow for milk, one sheep for wool, one pig for rashers, and we're going eat the hens,' I said, 'stuffed with the rest of the spuds.'

Their jaws were falling open as I slammed the door.

We never even had a pig.

Her head flies past me. I'm burning down Piggery Hill on my Chopper bike. I can hardly take a breath I'm going that fast, like a wild roller-coaster ride in a magazine, or in America. Next thing I'm looking down to see if it's safe to try to put my feet on the pedals, whizzing around like fire, when suddenly, there's Mam's head. Only her head, passing me out. No sign of her body. Mam's head, bowling along down the hill. She has her hair brushed real neat, and a nice silk scarf around her head, one with horses in a paddock on it. I always liked that scarf on her. I used to love looking at her putting it on in front of the big mirror in their room, if her and Da were going someplace special. I just liked the calm look of the horses or something. As she's passing by, I can hear her saying the 'Our Father'. She stops halfway through it and looks back at me as she's overtaking me, and does that thing where she talks without losing her place in the prayer.

'... Thy Kingdom come, Thy will be ... let you check round by my old home place, you know it makes me too sad to go there now ... done on earth as it is in Heaven, give us this day ... ' And she's away, the last words of the 'Our Father' lost as her head goes tumbling faster over bumps and potholes, and it's rounding the bend at the foot of Piggery Hill, out of sight, when I look up.

FOUR

WE HELD OUT FOR TWO DAYS. The rebels who freed Ireland from the English in 1916 only lasted for a week, and there was a lot more of them. I was on my own, because Mammy was half under a fairy spell, and she was mostly busy praying, which was kind of another spell, so she was under two spells at the same time. I think some of the rebels in 1916 were holy too, but they seemed to know when it was time to put down their rosary beads and their hurley sticks and pick up a rifle. Rosary beads are not much good in a war. Unless maybe it's a holy war, to see who can pray better.

I stored up all the cakes and the baking that the nosey neighbours and the fairies had made for us before I put up the barricade in the house. I did it at night, so it would catch them out when they came snooping around the next day. I put the table and chairs around inside the doors. I had to nail shut the windows with planks, which was hard because Da never let me use his good hammer and so I never had any practice. But I often saw the people in old Western films that we watched on Sunday afternoons doing it. The Virginian, he was one. The papa of the homestead would be trying to hold off the buckin' mad Indians until the Virginian arrived with help from town.

He'd move tables around, and hammer like mad, and tell everyone to stay down. The man's wife would have to learn in about two minutes how to fire a rifle for the first time ever, and the little children would all be bawling on the stairs. What the papa didn't know was that his best friend, who rode out to get help a few hours before, was lying only about a mile away with twenty arrows in his hide, and vultures were already eating his poor carcass. So no help was coming. Da didn't mind when the white man got scalped. He said the Indians were entitled to their land, and that they were only doing what the people in Ireland did when the English tried to grab our land off us.

I left a few gaps in the planks I hammered up, like the papa always did, where I could put Da's shotgun out. I could find just two cartridges for the gun, so I knew I would only be able to use it as a warning. Though I could kill at least two of them if I had to – maybe three – if I could get them close together. Or one behind another if they tried to rush through the front door all at once. I even knew what I'd say if they threatened to charge.

'Three of you aren't going to make it, so who's it going to be?' Da used to say that, pretending to be the papa in the film. It didn't really matter, though, because the Indians could only understand each other.

Mam seemed to think that praying would save us from everything, but I knew different. They tried every trick in the book.

'Will you let us in, JJ? We just want to see that you and your mother are alright.'

'Yep, we're grand. We're just having the dinner, thanks.'

'But ... '

'Mam is in the middle of a rosary for Da. Would you want to disturb her from that now, would you? And then we have twelve more rosaries to get through for different things, and we might just have time for a vigil before bed, if there's no further interruptions.'

Like I said, I was ready for them.

'But ... '

'Was there anything else?' I asked, as cool as you like.

There was a long silence, then a heavy knocking, and a man talking and pulling at the door handle.

'JJ, I want you to open up this door. That's enough of this auld carry-on now. Open the door and let Father Nealon and Dr Cassidy have a word with your mother, please, there's a good lad. We don't want to have to send for Guard Thompson below.'

I did what Mammy always told me to do when people are tormenting you, and I just ignored them.

Then they sent the women up to pray outside the door, hoping the excitement of hearing the rosary would be too much for Mammy, and make her tear the door off the hinges to get out and join them for a few of the Sorrowful Mysteries, and maybe a gallop through the Litany of the Saints. They knew she'd love that.

They set fresh bread and cakes outside for me to smell the baking, and then moved off a bit, crafty as you like, to see would I open up the door a crack to take them in. Sure, did they not know I often used the same trick to trap baby rabbits and fox cubs and wee birds and all the rest? A bit of bread or a bone under Da's old riddle, held up with a stick, with a length of string tied to it. Did they think I was a complete eejit altogether? They must have, but I wasn't. If the fairies were able to cod humans that easily, is it any wonder the Fairy Fort was packed to the rafters with dopes?

They even brought Spinner up to the door, whining and scratching to be let in, which was mean to poor Spinner, because that dog loved me so he did, and I loved him too, but I couldn't explain anything to him. He was just like the Indians – he could only understand his own kind. Then they put someone up on the roof, trying to get slates off or something, or to maybe come down the chimney. I left the shotgun standing up in the fire grate. All I had to do was put my finger on the trigger, and whoever was coming down the chimney would have more holes in him than a string vest.

I poked the barrel through the wooden planks now and then, just to let them know I meant business. Whenever I poked the gun out, the rosary would stop, but they'd start up again as soon as I took it back in.

'You forgot to say the Amen at the end of that last Holy Mary,' I said, the two barrels pointed at them. I think a few of the women would have liked it if I'd shot them; they'd have had something to talk about then. Or they could have become new statues in the church, with everyone looking up and praying to them. Then they'd finally know all their neighbours' secrets and sins. That was all they ever wanted out of life, to know their neighbours' business. That's what Da said anyway. 'They're only happy when they hear bad news about you,' he said.

I think the shotgun had them worried all right, because then Guard Thompson finally arrived up like the sheriff. The rosary stopped when he banged on the door. I don't think Guard Thompson minded too much about the rosary, because Da said he was a Protestant.

'Open the door now, PJ, and we'll say no more about it,' Guard Thompson shouted. He couldn't even get my name right.

'You go and say the rosary, and I might join in,' I said.

'Don't be a cheeky pup and open this door now, or by Christ I'll open it!'

I told him it was very bad – in fact it was a sin – to take the Lord's name in vain. He went off after that to get a sup of tea from his flask, and think about what to do next.

Then they started up the rosary again over near the barn, and Guard Thompson got into the squad car and banged the door shut.

Two days is a long time if you're not getting any sleep. I started to nod off at all sorts of times of the day and night. I'd wake with a jump, and get up and check out the gaps in the boards to see what was going on outside, and make a good bit of noise to let them know I was wide awake and ready for them.

Then, on the second night, I woke suddenly and my mother nearly had the door open. I jumped up and ran over to shut it, but they were all there, just outside, reaching in for her like hungry zombies I'd seen on telly one night when I was meant to be asleep. That was the only bit of that film I saw, but I still wet the bed after it. I pulled Mammy back, but she pushed me off. I couldn't believe she would help them against me. I grabbed her hair, and I bit her hand until there was blood on me and on her. She screamed the place down. I didn't blame her really, because I knew they had poisoned her mind with spells or lies or the apple tart or I don't know what. I couldn't hold her back, because I was tired and not as strong as usual. I grabbed the shotgun out of the fire and was going to blast the first one who came through the door, get three or four of them maybe, but then Uncle Patsy just rammed at the door with his thick shoulder and came in on top of us in a cloud of dust. The gun went off into the roof when I fell back. More people barged in then. Mam was bawling all the time, and I wondered why I hadn't just used the gun on me and her. That's what the papa in the Westerns said to his wife: 'If the sheriff don't get here, they ain't taking us.'

I could have grabbed the shotgun – there was one cartridge left in it – but Dr Cassidy stuck a big vet's needle into my arm, and Patsy was holding me and someone else was too, and I just screamed till everything went dark.

When I woke up, I was lying on a bench in Uncle Patsy's house, with a gang of them all around. I felt sick and sore and tired. I could see through the open door that Guard Thompson was sitting at the kitchen table, writing out pages of things. He had stacks of it already, but people were waiting their turn to tell him more stuff about me. Da was right, and they had plenty of bad news about me now. They were all so happy, they had even stopped praying.

Dr Cassidy came in and told me that Mammy had gone off somewhere quiet for a rest. Father Nealon told me that the fairies did not have my mother, and that there was no such thing as fairies to begin with. I tried to make him swear on it, because I still didn't believe him, but he told me that a priest can't go swearing about things. I was going to say that he didn't mind swearing that there was such a thing as angels, and they're just like fairies, but I didn't want to give Uncle Patsy another excuse to hit me. He'd nearly broken my arm in the house earlier, and he whispered to me when the priest and the doctor were out talking to Guard Thompson that he'd fix me if I tried any more 'funny business'. So I kept my mouth shut.

Father Nealon said that he was sure Uncle Patsy would take me to see my Mammy as soon as she was able for a visitor.

'So you can see your handiwork,' Uncle Patsy said.

I wanted to say, 'What about your handiwork, Uncle Patsy, robbing us blind?', but they were all getting ready to leave, and Uncle Patsy would not have long to wait for revenge if I did. So I kept my mouth shut again.

'That's if she ever wants to set eyes on you again,' Patsy said, seeing the priest out. 'She might as easy decide to get someone to drown you below in the river.'

He went out all holy and helpful with Father Nealon, Dr Cassidy and Guard Thompson. He put his head back in the door, and said that if I tried any stunts while he saw our visitors off, he'd make me rue the day I was born.

He was in the yard for a few minutes with the others, smoking and talking very low. Then the two cars left, Guard Thompson's and Dr Cassidy's, and Uncle Patsy came back into the house.

He stood over the bench, and I thought he was going to kill me there and then, strangle me or something, and just say I'd attacked him when they'd all gone. He had an evil look in his eye and brown spit, like dry stout I used to see on Da's lips sometimes, at the corners of his mouth. But he just stood looking at me.

'Oh, you're your father's son alright,' he said, and went back out to the yard.

Well, who else's son did he think I was?

FIVE

THE BEST TIME TO HAVE A siege if you're an Irish rebel might be at Easter, because Jesus died and rose again then, and the 1916 Rising was at Easter. But I didn't think God or Jesus was doing any good for my family, even though Mammy had prayed non-stop for months and months. Da was still gone, and now she was gone too. So that was part of the reason that I'd decided on a siege in June. It was also because the days are longer then, and I wanted to be able to see what the enemy was up to at night. But mostly it just happened to be in June when I finally got fed up to my back teeth with the whole ragtag lot of them.

Like many other Irish rebels after losing a siege, I had a spell in jail. Some of the English I know were pretty bad when they caught Irish rebels, but none of the ones I ever heard of were as bad as my Uncle Patsy was to me. I didn't mind so much having to work all summer long on his farm, or even being larruped by him when I wasn't fast enough for his liking, but he didn't take me to see Mammy every two weeks, like he promised Father Nealon he would. He took me when he felt like it, which wasn't often, and I saw her only three times that whole summer.

Our old neighbour Phil Reilly, from down near the lake, was out in the fields one day at the end of the summer. He saw his dog Spinner sniffing a giant mushroom. That's what he thought it was at first, he said afterwards. Then Phil went closer. He wanted to know what his dog found so interesting about a mushroom. It turned out not to be a mushroom, but the big white skull of a dead person. In fact, it was the first piece of my da to come out of hiding, nearly a year after he'd gone in, though, of course, nobody knew for sure who it belonged to at that time.

After the forensics fellas from Dublin identified it as a human skull, half the gardaí in Ireland, led by Guard Thompson from the town, came down to Phil Reilly's field. They were all in their big wellies and rubber gloves like the vet, and big boiler suits like the mechanic, and with sniffer dogs and slash hooks. And boys, did they slash!

They cleared thistles, nettles, rushes, scutch grass, bushes, bulrushes, ferns, saplings and briars from all the fields and ditches. They lifted rocks and tree trunks, and prodded and poked the ground. The poor rabbits must have thought the end of the world was coming. The gardaí looked for any fresh marks where they had been digging, but they found no sign of a grave. They couldn't for the life of them figure out where the skull had come from, or where the rest of the fella it belonged to was. Neither could I for that matter. Spinner couldn't have eaten every last scrap of a whole human being, except for the bones of the skull, now could he? He was far too skinny to have eaten a whole person on his own. Anyhow, me and Spinner were best pals, so I knew he was innocent. He would just not eat a human being.

In the end they tried to get the sniffer dogs to ask Spinner, in their own language, to show them where exactly he'd found the skull, because he might have dragged it into Phil's field from someplace else.

Phil Reilly's dog never had such gas in all his life. Spinner took off across the fields with all the sniffer dogs hot on his heels, all snuffling and wagging and whimpering like it was lambing time and they were on the loose for the weekend. Spinner ran and ran and ran, and he didn't stop until he came to the river.

The River Weal is shallow at the sides but fast in the middle. Spinner stood on a low muddy part of the bank where the cattle went to drink, barking at the fast-flowing water in the middle. This was a favourite game of his. That's because in the summer I'd often go down there with him and have a swim. I'd go into the river farther up, sit in an inflated old tractor tube, and let the fast current carry me downstream until the water got shallow and I'd run aground on the stony shore. Spinner would run alongside me down the riverbank, barking like a crazy mad mutt of a hound, which is exactly what he was doing when all the garda sniffer dogs finally joined him.

By the time all the young gardaí caught up with them, puffing from the heat in their big uniforms, the sniffer dogs were rolling in cow-flops and playing chasing, and Spinner was still barking at the middle of the river. He was waiting for the tractor tube to come bombing down with my white legs hanging out over the side. The Sergeant had stayed back at the house, and when his car radio announced what had happened, and mentioned the cow-dung and all, he said those dogs weren't worth a blasted curse, that they had the station house destroyed, and what for, and he banged the door of the squad car like my da used to sometimes bang our kitchen door.

The frog-gardaí searched the river anyway. They found two old sacks of stones in a deep pool at a bend in the river, with hair and bones of drowned pups or kittens in them, but no sign of any more human bones. They found a lot of fishing line too, with lead weights on it and rusty hooks in the reeds, and a bubble float and two copper spinners. Probably most of them were mine. Me and Da were the only people who ever fished there.

'Them lead weights and spinners cost,' Da used to say whenever I'd lose one in them weeds, or get snagged on a rock.

Anyway, I took them, even though they were rusty, because the gardaí didn't seem to think any of that stuff would help them with their investigation, as they started calling it.

A few days later a different neighbour found a bit of a jawbone in another field. They couldn't find the whole jaw, and the neighbour said it was probably because a fox or something had got at it. Poor Spinner wasn't getting as many pats now as he used to. The forensic lads eventually said it was almost definitely part of the skull they already had, and not a bit of some other person. I don't know what people would have done if it had turned out there was another skull knocking about the place.

When no other bones were found after a few more days, the gardaí all went home. Nothing more happened for a few weeks. Nobody knew who the skull and the jaw belonged to. Guard Thompson said they were doing tests on them, but it would take a long time, and it would be a big help if they had the rest of the lad the skull belonged to.

Then September and October started having an arm-wrestling match, back and forth, but October was winning. There was a wild windy night, and Phil Reilly was out again the day after the storm, checking if any of his fences were broken, or his animals maybe injured or lost, or blown onto the wrong farm. He found a long white bone not far from where Spinner had found the skull. The forensics boys were back like a shot. They examined it for a while, and finally they said it was a human leg bone, and that it probably belonged to the same lad that owned the skull and the jaw. They brought the leg bone to an old cell at the station, where the other bits were still waiting to be put together, and they started to match them all up. It was like a jigsaw taking shape.

'And don't for God's sake let any clown bring them cursed dogs near this cell, or that'll be an end to this investigation,' the Sergeant said.

This time there were gardaí everywhere. They went back over old ground. The rabbits took a holiday. On the second day of the new search one young garda started climbing trees. He went up a few trees around the place, and came down shaking his head. Then finally he decided to go up a big pine cone tree that had been there for as long as anyone could remember. He had a rope but he still needed a bunt up because the pine didn't have any good branches lower down for climbing. It took him a good while, but once he got up to the green branches, he vanished altogether.

They must have known they were getting warm this time, because they sent for Uncle Patsy to come down to the field. He'd brought me with him, to keep an eye on me. He forgot to mention to the gardaí that he'd told me he'd break my neck if I so much as opened my mouth or made one false move. One of the frog-gardaí had taken off his goggles and his flippers, and he was now a tree-climber garda. He was up the tree for ages, but you could see from outside how high up he was going, because some branches were shaking. I was thinking that the big tree would be a good spot to hide in if you could only get up there. Then the garda said something from the middle of the tree on his walkie-talkie to the Sergeant, who was beside me and Uncle Patsy, and the Sergeant said, 'Jesus. Oh Jesus Christ of Almighty!' and he looked up at the tree.

I thought maybe he had caught Mam's praying disease. Walkie-talkies were all going like mad then, and everyone gathered under the pine tree, looking up. It was a bit like the little novena prayer Mammy had from Lourdes or one of those holy places, with all the children in a circle looking up at Our Lady, who was telling them a big secret. Except it was all the gardaí looking up this time, and I was the only child there.

Then they closed off all around the bottom of the tree with a big curtain, like they were going to have a Punch and Judy show at two o'clock. They put a scaffold on the bare bottom part, with planks on it. I hadn't a clue what was going on. Was Jesus in the tree, coming down personally to ask all the women in the town to stop tormenting Him with prayers? I wouldn't have blamed Him. Or maybe God Himself was in the tree, come to tell my mam that He hadn't a blue clue where my da was, and to please stop asking and asking and asking. And to call off the neighbours too, please.

'Maybe they found an eagle's nest,' I said, but even Uncle Patsy had the rosary beads out by then, and he didn't hear, or let on he didn't hear a word I said. He hardly ever said any prayers, so he couldn't do Mammy's 'just give me a minute' trick. Uncle Patsy mostly had rosary beads so he could take them out if Father Nealon was expected for a visit. Uncle Patsy would watch for the priest coming up the lane, and he'd take out the beads and make me kneel down alongside him. Then he'd act all surprised when Father Nealon would come in at the back door.

'Ahhh, Father, you're very welcome! We were just finishing up the rosary. Come on in.'

Patsy didn't even know the rosary, just bits of a few of the prayers from his school days: 'Hail Holy Queen, Mother of Mercy ... let not our sins and transgressions now cause us to falter ... turn then most gracious advocate thine eyes of mercy towards us ... aaahhhh Father, we were just finishing up the rosary, come in, come in, come in.'

Sure enough when I looked around, there was Father Nealon tramping up the lane and in at the back door. Cute enough of Uncle Patsy to spot the priest before anyone else, and get out his beads.

Did eagles eat people? I knew they ate sheep, or at least lambs, because I'd heard they did once or twice on the farms near us, but that was going back a long time, because farmers shot them all. I never saw an eagle. Da said they had one in Dublin Zoo, and that that was the proper place for them.

The forensic lads all started to go up the tree. There was so many of them in the tree, I heard a few cracks from branches, and a couple of them had to come back down fast. Three or four gardaí stayed in the field, in case any eagle egg-robbers came sniffing around. The rest of them went off for their tea.

You're caught! It was some game of hide-and-seek, all right. It took the gardaí, a whole station full of them, and reinforcements from all over the county, nearly a year to find my da, all of him, in the end.

We never actually said the big pine tree was out of bounds, but considering all the other carry-on of my da, I suppose we really should have. Sure, how could I have got up there? I was only ten when that game started. I was still too small to climb the tree when they found him, and by then I was eleven and a half. Look at all the help that big tall garda needed to get himself up. My da did it though. Got way up.

I heard some of them talking.

'He had a big tow rope. He must have been very determined to do it this time.'

Clever enough of him – he pulled the rope up after him, not to leave any clues, or evidence, as the gardaí liked to call it. After the gardaí had a whisper with Uncle Patsy for about ten minutes, they came over to me. They told me my da must have got stuck or wedged in where the high-up branches are all jammed real tight together. 'Slipped, or fell a bit or something,' the Sergeant with the red face said.

'How do you know that a bunch of old bones is my da?' I asked the Sergeant. Uncle Patsy told me not to be a smart aleck, and I'd have felt the back of his hand only for the police were beside us.

The Sergeant said that when my da went missing he was wearing the same clothes as the lad in the tree. 'And one or two things in his pockets made it easy to identify him,' he said. 'A big wind shook him I'd say – a big sudden gust of wind, like the one that was blowing the day they found all his ... him.'

Then the Sergeant went back to town with his big bag of bones, to finish the jigsaw.

So up he went, my da, and there he sat, or stood, kind of, for nearly a whole year, just waiting to be found.

At least he had something to drink for a while, because I heard a garda saying there was a bottle in his old jacket pocket, even after all that time. Da was cute enough. He knew he was going to be hiding for a long while, and he must have brought a supply of food and something to drink with him up the tree. Sure, you couldn't be getting up and down a big yoke of a tree like that every hour or two when you'd be hungry.

And he was clever enough to be able to think of leaving us a message too, even at the very end, because he put some kind of a note into the bottle when it was empty, and wrote my name and Mam's name on it. Then he signed it, which was one of the main ways they were sure it was really Da after all. I'm not sure exactly what he said in it, because I never saw the note. Father Nealon saw it.

'He said that he just wanted you to know that he loved you and your mother very much.'

'Is that all?' I said. 'Sure, we knew that!'

It's not usually where you think of finding a message – in a bottle up in a tree, in the pocket of a jacket that's holding your da's bones together.

They kept calling it 'the remains', but there wasn't any remains left at that stage. Da was all gone, except the clothes he had on. They even gave Mammy a little lock of his hair, which I didn't think looked like the colour of Da's hair at all, but it seems there were still a few bits of it clinging to something, I'm not sure what. It wasn't his head, because Spinner found that. Maybe it was on his shoulders, like it was when he'd sit in the middle of the kitchen floor and Mam would cut his hair for him. Then she'd cut mine too, real short and a bit too tight. When she was finished my hair, Da would look at me and say something like, 'I hope you got the registration number of the combine harvester that did that to your head,' and I'd say, 'You're not one to talk, skinner,' and he'd grab the scissors off the table and chase me out into the yard, shouting, 'Come here to me. I think your mother missed a bit.'

Dr Cassidy said the sun and the rain might change the colour of hair a bit too. They gave the hair to my mother at the hospital where she was having her big rest. They put it into one of those envelopes I used to get my school reports posted in, the ones with the little clear plastic window on the front. I thought of my da getting an A+ in his Hiding Exam.

Then I got to thinking about something far more serious. I thought: how is Da going to come now and get Mammy out of that hospital, where she'd been having the longest rest ever recorded in history since Snow White? The only reason I'd stayed all summer in Uncle Patsy's house, apart from the fact that he said he'd break my back if I ran away, helping him with his farm, as well as minding our own farm when I could, was just to wait till Da would be back.

Then Da would collect Mammy and me, and we could all go home and be together as a family again. I don't think Uncle Patsy knew what to do next either, because he started being even more bad-tempered with me for every little thing I did wrong. He belted me now for no reason at all a good few times, and even started to make me sleep in the barn when I didn't get all my work done to suit him.

So that's when I had to really decide what was the best thing for me to do. If I ran away and Uncle Patsy caught me, he'd welt hell out of me. But he was starting to do that anyway, so I thought I might as well make a run for it and see how far I could get. At least if I was caught, I'd know what I was being welted for.

What I really needed to do was to find a good place to hide, and try to figure out what to do next. I couldn't plan anything with Uncle Patsy breathing stale porter down my neck.

A scarecrow is walking across the fields. The thing is, he has no head. His head is after falling off, and the rest of him doesn't seem to notice or care. The tin head is on the ground, and his big white gloss-painted eyes with a black middle are staring at a mud-ball. The scarecrow's body is carrying a big blackthorn stick. Suddenly he stops in the middle of a field full of cattle. I think maybe he's noticed that his head is not where it should be, and maybe he'll go back for it. Then the stick goes up in the air, and the scarecrow begins to sort of conduct the cows. They all look up and just stare silently for a minute or two, except for chewing away on the cud all the time. The scarecrow gently waves his stick like it's a magic wand. The cows take a deep breath, and then start to moo, deep down into the grass. The moo sound travels underground and comes up in the next field. In the field where it comes up, a flock of crows puffs up over the ditch, whooshed up by the lowing and mooing travelling under them. The lowing wafts them gently towards some bare trees. They settle on the branches like little music notes.

I hear someone calling my name and I open my eyes to see if it's the headless conductor scarecrow.

SIX

T HAT SKULL MIGHT HAVE HAD THEM all puzzled down below, but the crows knew what it was. Sure I bet they couldn't believe their luck. A whole human being, wedged so tight it couldn't move to swish them away, stuck up in their very own tree! The same lad who used to blow them all to bits in a flash with his shotgun, and then hang their corpses upside down on sticks, their black beaks glued together with a big blob of hard blood to frighten the rest away. And now there he was, up in their favourite tree, with no gun to fire at them.

I bet they had a crow festival with my da. Watching him alive at first, them hopping slowly closer and closer, like vultures, waiting for the wind to send them a telegram. Then, after waiting and waiting, at last the feast started. They'd wake up at the crack of dawn, and eat an eye out, or a bit of purple tongue, or a cheek, or whatever they could peck without having to stir themselves too much. They have strong stomachs, crows. Strong beaks too. I've looked at them, dead ones on the road. A few times I got one in the jaws of a rat trap, caught trying to rob the rasher rind Da set in it. Rob the eye out of your head. Out of your da's head. Jackdaws, crows, scald crows, rooks, even magpies, all having a go off my poor da.

Then one of them discovers meat on the fingers, exposed at the end of the sleeves, gorged with old blood from hanging, dangling down there for days or weeks, like the big purple head on a turkey in the barn before Christmas, upside down, with the cat looking up at it, licking its lips. Or the vultures, having a feed on the poor lad full of arrows who never made it back to town to fetch the sheriff. Cured now like ham. So many scrabbling round his head, you can't see what they're eating, just a mass of wings and feathers and those strong black beaks pulling at strings of what they can get. The same stuff we're all made of. Then eventually the head tilting back far enough to let them drill down into the neck, into the circle of the collar of the shirt. Like those sweets I used to sometimes get, where you bend the little plastic man's head back, and a sweet like a tiny bar of soap comes out of his neck. Standing in a ring round the collar of his shirt like they were on the rim of a big cooking pot.

'What's for dinner? Caw caw.'

'Remember the human crow-killer? Caw.'

'Murderer. Caw.'

'Well, we're having his guts. Caw caw caw caw.'

Then they all join in on the big joke: 'Caw caw caw caw caw caw caw caw caw caw caw caw caw caw caw caw caw.'

Da for dinner, disappearing in big frantic gulps down their oily, bulging, feathery necks. Then some of the bastard birds become so sick full, they'd have to get away and let in others waiting to eat. The full ones, they'd go and preen Da's blood into their wings, and shit a white splat of some part of Da down through the branches. Maybe they shat some of Da onto our house, and we never knew. A bit with his wedding ring, or a fingernail, or a tooth or a filling in it.

I wonder if the crows were able to hop down then, right down into his chest, when the meat and windpipe and Adam's apple and veins were all pulled away from round his neck like spaghetti. They are nosey birds, and cheeky enough to try anything. Why stop, when you can see more meat down the hole you just made, even if the opening is a wee bit narrow? Soon fix that anyway – just eat more off the edges. Fish can do it if they find a body of a dead sheep or a fox underwater. They just move in, and stay inside till they've eaten their way back out again. Eat themselves out of house and home.

The crows going at it in relays inside Da's white belly, black as coal miners. I'd say it helped them get through the winter, between the wet and the frost and the snow. It's a hungry time for birds and animals. Stripped back to the spine and the ribs, arse and all pecked out. Down, down, down. How far down? To the legs, the top of his thighs.

Tops of the thighs! That's funny. Well, sort of. My mam said they first met at a competition called *The Tops of the 'Towns'*, a kind of a variety show where people got up on a stage and sang or told corny jokes.

'Next act up on the stage, ladies and gentlemen, is Mr Tom Sheridan! What will you be doing for us tonight, Tom?'

'Thanks, Seamus. I'd like to do a little song I wrote myself called "I Can't Sit Down Since Them Crows Ate My Arse".'

How far down did they get? I wonder. Not much left for the bluebottles when they finally got past the crows, fat as ticks and half-dead themselves from gluttony. But then they don't need a lot. A little bit goes a long way with the flies. A pinkie finger would probably feed a whole bluebottle family for a month. Or a willie and balls. Yes. I don't really like to think of anything eating my da's private parts, but I'm pretty sure they were gone with the rest when they found him, so something made short work of them.

In the summer sometimes I'd hear Da yelling up in a field that he was being eaten alive by flies. They got him in the end. I think sheep bring more flies than cows or even pigs. I bet my da brought a good few flies up to that tree, high up and all as it was. I wonder did I ever rest under the tree while Da was up there, becoming remains? Maybe he was still alive, trying to say my name, but with no tongue, or only part of it left. Things could have been falling out of him, and on top of me, while I was sheltering there from a downpour of rain, and I never knew.

'Hello, son. You can try a few of these maggots the next time you go fishing. The trout will think it's Christmas.'

Then when the weather picked up a bit, the swallows came after all the newly-hatched flies, and the hawks hunted the swallows, and the blue tits and the robins gorged themselves on the maggots that lost their balance and fell off Da, and dropped down lower into the tree.

On the boy sitting in out of the rain.

The fox came for the odd blind scaldie that fell out of a nest, trying to fly too soon and crash-landing, and wound up sitting at the bottom of the tree, terrified out of its wits, keeping as still as possible, hoping not to be sniffed out by the wrong animal.

All that from my da.

Looking back, I'd say by the end of that winter there wasn't a big lot of him left, barring the clean bones and that bit of hair. And his clothes, of course. Then the flies came along and did some spring-cleaning. The crows and flies very nearly committed the perfect crime, clearing away all the evidence, but I know they were all in on it.

Who could blame them? It's not every day they'd find a whole human buried in the air. The clothes and the branches held him all together, the big garda said. They kept his bones, not where they should be in a body exactly, but sort of around the right position at least. And they kept them up in the tree long enough for the crows to clear off, and to get away from the scene of the crime.

Maybe he would have liked himself all hollowed out like that. He could have poured all the beer in Maguire's Public Bar down into himself then, which is what Mammy said one time is all he wanted to do.

Instead, he just sat there, empty and quiet. So quiet he could have been nested in. Tomtits might have moved into his skull – in and out of his eye sockets with dry moss and sheep's wool, and little feathers, maybe even a few wisps of his own hair, to put a soft lining in the nest for their little scaldies. A door in and a door out. Left eye in, and right eye out. My da mostly liked the little birds, as long as they didn't go around eating his cabbage, so maybe they liked him too. The crows sure did.

But even with his jaw all hanging down, I wonder was he really quiet, like there was nothing left to be said? I wonder what the sound was like in the breeze, or what song did my father sing when the wind was howling through his skull? A banshee cry?

For nearly a full year his best Sunday jacket held him up straight in a pine tree, out of the sight and smell of everyone.

They searched all over after he vanished, but they never looked up.

SEVEN

'I'M NOT HAVING A LAZY PUP on this farm.' Pray for us. 'Lazy pups wind up in the river.' Pray for us. 'You're a useless runt like your waster of a father.' Pray for us. 'You'll get tough quick where you are now, me bucko.' Pray for us.

'No medals for crying around this place.' Pray for us. 'Only for you're my sister's own flesh and blood.' Pray for us. 'I should have welted some good out of you before now.' Pray for us.

'But by jaysus I'll knock the corners off you, so I will, God help me.' Pray for us.

'I'll tear that shirt off you and hang it on a stick in the field.' Pray for us.

'After the hens are shut in, bring a lock of turf for the fire.' Pray for us.

'Now and in our final hour. Amen.'

Uncle Patsy's house was small and dark inside, except for a little red light that never went out under a big scary picture of the Sacred Heart. You could see right through the Sacred Heart's chest to His heart, which was dripping blood. I wondered if this was what happened when someone's heart was scalded. Mam often used to say that we had her heart scalded. I didn't like to think of Mam's heart dripping blood like that.

The bulb was too weak for the Sacred Heart to be able to see what was going on in that house, though, because if the Sacred Heart saw the half of it, He would have come down off the wall and kicked Uncle Patsy all the way to Hell. Even on sunny days it always felt cold in the house, and there was a queer smell too, like a mousetrap that someone forgot to empty.

Uncle Patsy kept a lot of old newspapers everywhere. He had old newspapers on the floor, to soak up things that got spilled. He had them at the back door, to soak the water that came in at the bottom of the door when it rained. The bottom of the door was rotten and, even when it was closed, it still felt like it was open. He used old newspapers for a table cover, and he had more newspapers ripped up and stuck on a nail, for your business in the toilet.

The toilet was in a little shed in the yard. The flusher didn't work, so you had to flush the toilet with a bucket of water from the tap in the yard. Filling it reminded me of my da going to wee in the middle of the night.

'There's a snake in there. Mind it doesn't bite your arse,' Uncle Patsy would say if I met him when he'd be coming out of the toilet, and I knew it needed flushing after him. I tried to just keep going in the field or the ditch myself, so as to leave him to do his own flushing, but he never did it himself. He noticed everything.

'Too lazy to shite now are you? I'm up to your tricks, oh yes me bucko! You can wipe your arse with nettles if you like, but you keep that jacks clear, do you hear me? Your Uncle Patsy didn't come down the river on a bicycle. Now get that bucket and flush out the bowl till it's spotless.'

Sometimes he'd roll up a newspaper and wallop me around the place if a cow got through a gap in the ditch, saying it was my fault. Or if I broke an egg, bringing them in from the roost in the barn. I didn't let him know about wetting the bed. I copied his own trick with newspapers, and put old papers under the sheet, to keep the damp out of the mattress.

I often wanted to say something back, but I was too afraid of him then, and I didn't want to give him any excuse to go back to Mam and complain about me. If I said the wrong thing, or if I didn't do my work the way he liked it done, he'd tell me I'd never see her again. I saw her little enough over those woeful months as it was, and I was thinking all the time that the only way to remedy that was to get me and her back together in our own house for good, where nobody could tell us what to do. But I still badly wanted to say something, to let Uncle Patsy know that he would not get away with what he was doing for ever. My da always told me not to be afraid to speak my mind, so I practised what I would say, for when the time was right. Once I had started to practise, though, I just had to get it said, and I forgot all about waiting till the time would be right. Anyway, when is the time ever right to tell someone that you hate their guts?

One day Uncle Patsy came in in a terrible fury, the worst I'd seen him in for a long while. He was after adding another dent to his old van, trying to avoid a calves in the lane while he was coming up to the house. It wasn't all that bad of an accident, and I'd say he'd lost money in the betting shop. He had drink taken too, because he had eyes like a sheep going to slaughter.

'I'm after taking the corner off the gatepost, trying to avoid that cursed beast. How did it get into the lane, that's what I'd like to know? Would you tell me that now, ha? But sure how would you know, and you sitting in here, warming your hole on the range all day, ha, with your little girl's hands on you? Were you afraid you'd get a blister, were you, if you did a bit of man's work? I'll blister you, you useless little runt. Pity it wasn't you standing beyond in the lane, you no-good bloody waster, for if it was, I'd have gone straight ahead, and saved the van and the gatepost itself.'

I saw the flat of his open hand coming, and then I was on the kitchen floor with my ear ringing, like someone had fired a shotgun beside my head.

'You have your mother's heart broken, you useless get. Well, you'll not stop in this house, for I know the place that will soften your cough, me buck.'

He went on ranting out of him. He made me nearly cry by saying that about Mammy's heart being broken, but I fought hard and held back the tears. I can't remember all he said, because on top of the ringing in my ear, there was a bit of blood coming out. So I decided there and then that it was as good a time as any to tell Uncle Patsy what I thought of him, for a change. 'Maybe if you didn't spend so much time getting the names of horses out of the newspapers and losing money, and more time fixing the big holes in them fences of yours, then maybe your cows wouldn't be always getting out on you. And, anyway, half of them cows are ours, because you took them and never paid for them, which is really the same as stealing, and it's our money you're losing in the betting shop. I wonder what your great friend Father Nealon would think if he knew you were a thief and a fibber, as well as a lazy thick who can't even flush away his own jobbies.'

Some things that I hadn't practised at all started to come out then too, because Uncle Patsy was just standing there with his mouth open, not sure what to do. He wasn't hitting me, so I kept going.

'Maybe that's why nobody would ever marry you, because you're nothing but a mean hoor. My da even said it. He said,

"That Patsy fella, if he owned Scandinavia he wouldn't give you a slide." He said you were as tight as a heifer's arse going up a hill, and he said you were a malignant something, and I know that's exactly the right name, because I even wrote it down so I wouldn't forget. It's on a piece of paper under my mattress above in the old house to this day. And I can see now that my da was being too nice about you.'

Well, after that, and some other things I can't remember now, Uncle Patsy sort of regained his senses. He picked up a stick he kept at the door for hooshing cattle up the lane. He didn't say anything, just came at me with it over his head like a Viking who was having some sort of a nervous breakdown. I took a few sods of turf from the pile I'd brought in, and I pegged them at him. I got him on the side of the head with one big heavy wet one. That slowed him up for a minute, and I ran under the table and straight out the back door.

I kept running till I couldn't breathe properly any more. My heart was trying to get out through my mouth so it could find a quieter place to live. The bones were gone out of my legs too. I was running so hard and for so long, I think I knocked them up into my back someplace. If a man-eating tiger had escaped from the zoo, and got the train down to our farm, I would have been the easiest meal he ever caught. In a way, I'd have preferred if a man-eating tiger had caught me. At least it would have been all over in one big gulp. But in the end it was a drunk, mad uncle that caught me.

He found me after half an hour, drunk as he was. He knew all the hiding places around his own farm and fields, and I didn't, because I'd worked so hard on his farm all summer that I was always too exhausted to go exploring when all the work was done. I thought I'd run halfway to Dublin, but I didn't get that far. I didn't really have anywhere proper to run to anyway. When he found me, he was more mad than I'd ever seen him, or anyone else, and he beat the living daylights out of me in the field. I didn't have the energy to fight back this time. I didn't even have the energy to say the 'I Confess to Almighty God' prayer that people sometimes say when they think they're going to die. Da said that even the auld pagans should learn that prayer off and have it handy, just in case.

'You've had this coming a long time, ye little ungrateful scrawny whelp's bastard!' he said. I thought Uncle Patsy just might die before he got to the end of the sentence, because he was in such a pure rage. His face was like a pan of black pudding, but he was a hardy farmer, and he wasn't near finished.

'Your poor mother had enough to put up with having one waster in that house, without you starting to do the big fella as well. And she just might be starting to come right at last herself. I'll straighten you out though, me bucko. I'll knock the corners off ye so I will, I will for sure. And I'll see to it that that poor woman doesn't have to look at your cheeky puss again either.'

Then more kicks and wallops, and belts of the fat stick, and God knows what else, in case I didn't believe him the first forty or fifty times. I never knew I had corners, but I was sure I could feel them coming off me right enough. He said a lot of other things too, mostly stuff that I can't remember, because I was in bad pain where he'd kicked me. I felt for the first time in my life that my own heart was scalded and I thought that if I ever really made my own mother feel that way, then I surely was sorry. On the way home we met Guard Thompson coming along on the road.

'What happened to this buck?' Guard Thompson asked.

'Climbing a tree, Guard. Anything to get away from his books and his study. I don't want the lad to wind up at the land like myself, but sure he never opens a book. Out acting the go-boy like a recently deceased we won't mention. Only I saw what he was at and managed to break his fall a bit, sure he would have split his skull surely. Well, I can't be responsible for this fella's welfare any more. Didn't he already put his own mother in the mental hospital?'

Then Uncle Patsy said that I had even threatened to kill him when he was 'rescuing' me. Well, I did threaten to kill him, after he said that about my da. I only said it in a whisper, like a prayer, but he had ears like a black hoor of a bat, and he heard me. Or maybe he was going to say that anyway, just to make me look like a dangerous madman. I didn't think about the mental hospital part of what he'd said till a lot later.

Uncle Patsy even said I'd been mitching off school since September, though it was really him that kept me away from school, to do work on the farm. He told me himself at the beginning of school term that since I was going to be staying in his house, I'd be earning my keep with real work, and not reading books. I don't know what he was worrying about, because I never had any time to read. I never saw such a thing as a book in Uncle Patsy's house anyway, only squares of old newspapers on a rusty nail in the outhouse.

EIGHT

I KNEW THE CARE STAFF WOULD find me eventually. They always did, but I liked to annoy them as often as I could, and for as long as I could. There were only so many places to hide in the home Uncle Patsy and Father Nealon and Dr Cassidy eventually put me into. Mammy would never have allowed them to do a thing like that – to lock me away in a children's home, like I was a poor orphan or something. But Mammy was still trying to finish having a rest in the hospital, and she probably didn't even know they were after doing it. I asked Father Nealon why Uncle Patsy had said that my mother was in a mental hospital, and the priest said there was a mental part of the hospital all right, but that Mammy had just had a few tests there, and then went back to the normal part again.

I tried to explain, and tell the truth. When they brought me to the children's home first, I told them it was all a pack of lies about me, made up mostly by my Uncle Patsy, who should have been in the mental part of the hospital all the time, and that he was backed up in the lies by Father Nealon and Dr Cassidy, for a reason I couldn't ever figure out. But when adults decide to gang up on an eleven-year-old, the adults always, always win. They swap lies like Green

Shield stamps, and they all agree with each other, and back each other up in their lies, and add more lies every second like a bluebottle laying eggs, and make the lies bigger, and basically do whatever they like to you. They could kill you with lies and then say it was just a terrible, terrible accident, and they'd get away with it once enough of them were in on it. Then they all go off saying good morning to priests and nuns and bishops and police and teachers and anyone else holy or important, as if they were all saints, just doing God's work.

'Patsy?'

'Yes. Who's this?'

'This is God here, Patsy. I have a little job I'd like you to do for me.'

'God! Of course, God, anything You like! What is it You need?'

'That young lad?'

'Yes, God. JJ. He's a bit of a bosthoon. Wants a good kick in ... sorry God, I'm jumping the gun. What did You have in mind?'

'Not at all, that's bang on. You have the idea, Patsy! Knock the tar out of the little beggar, and keep knocking it out of him till he's fit for the Kingdom of God.'

'No sooner said, God ... ! Consider it done!'

So I knew then that I had to get smart to beat them. I had to get cunning. If I could be even half as sly as they made me out to be, then I'd have the last laugh on them all. Like the times I'd hear the men back home, when they'd be hunting rabbits, saying, 'We have him, we nearly have him!' If those big balubas thought they nearly had me, well, they nearly had no such thing.

The children's home was called St Somebody's, a big Irish name none of the boys could pronounce. I think the staff there thought that if they all smiled enough at me, and told me how much they all cared about me, then I wouldn't want to leave. For the first couple of weeks they really believed it was working, because I was not trying to run away or do anything against the rules. But that was only because my ribs, my back, my left arm and both my legs were all still sore from when Uncle Patsy had tried to murder me in cold blood in the field. I couldn't figure out how many minders worked in St Somebody's, because every day there were different staff going in and out.

There were four other boys like me living there, so between all the pains I had and all the strangers coming and going including a nurse who kept an eye on my injuries, it suited me to just keep my mouth shut for the first few weeks. Only one of the other boys, Egg was his nickname, was friendly to me at first. He gave me two posters to stick on my bedroom wall, since I didn't have anything to put up, and all the other children had stuff on their walls.

It was the first time I ever got to stick a picture that wasn't of Jesus on my wall. One poster was of a horse, 'because you're a culchie from bogland and you probably like horses,' Egg said. The other poster was of a football team, Manchester United.

'Because the Red Devils rule.'

Egg loved Manchester United, but it turned out he really liked horses too. He told me he could ride bareback, and that him and his friends even kept horses where he was from in Dublin. He couldn't believe it when I told him I'd never even sat up on a horse in my life.

'And how do yez get around in bogland then, to the shop an' all?' he wanted to know.

'Cars,' I said.

Not very many people had cars where Egg lived, he said, but nearly everyone had a horse.

'That's mad,' he said. 'Youse have no horses, and we've hardly no cars.'

Egg and me were friends straight away, and that made my first few weeks in that home a bit better. I used to laugh a lot at the funny way he said things, and his funny Dublin accent. I think I made Egg laugh too. He protected me against the other boys, or one of them at least, who was a big bully. His name was Marko. He did all kinds of things to torment me, but when he tore my Manchester United poster and said that the team was shite, Egg turned into a red devil himself, and he plastered Marko to the floor. Marko was crying in the end, and the nurse had to put some stuff on his eye. He never annoyed me again. Egg was always in a lot of trouble over fighting, though, and he didn't get to go on many outings, like to swimming or the pictures.

I got to know a few of the names of the staff, but not many. I didn't try to remember them because I wasn't planning on staying there long. Still, they tried to have these little chats with me about my family. Egg warned me about 'the little chats'.

'Tell them to fuck off,' he said.

Egg's language was a holy fright, as my mother would say, but I kind of liked it.

Whenever we had free time, I used to wander around the grounds, looking for an escape tunnel through the fence that went all the way round the place. When I went hiding in trees, I was really looking for which road to follow when I finally escaped. I also wanted them not to think I was gone, only hiding, to give myself a good head start on them.

Hallowe'en came but nobody dressed up except the staff. We had our school in St Somebody's, so it didn't really feel like a proper school holiday then, because we were still in the same place.

They had this thing called a conference. Everyone who lived in the home had to have at least one. A conference was just one of the nosey little chats the staff loved having, only it was far longer than usual, and had adults who didn't even work in the home at it too, as well as experts in making children behave themselves. As the first few weeks went by, I discovered that they loved having those conferences. Eventually my turn came to have one. A case conference, the staff said it was called, and I was the star of it.

'It's your turn to be the fucking case,' Egg said.

One boy, the youngest lad in Somebody's, thought it was where you got to go in and tell the staff what you wanted, like going to see Santy. I didn't know his real name – he was just called Mouse. Mouse didn't understand that a conference was where the staff told you what they wanted.

'Well, well, well, if it isn't little Mouse! And what would you like for Christmas this year, little Mouse, eh?'

'I'd like an Action Man, a case conference, and a surprise.'

One thing is for sure – it kept all those staff busy, arranging conferences about children. The staff could buy nice cakes for themselves, and make huge pots of tea and coffee for all the experts they invited along, to show them how great they were at minding other people's children. They weren't any good at it at all, but, like I said, if adults get in on a big lie together, you can't win if you're the child stuck in the middle of the lie.

Those staff, though, most of them couldn't mind mice, big or small, and they especially couldn't mind their own business. I never asked any of the staff if their mam was happy, or shouted at them if they were bold, or if their dad ever walloped them. I didn't ever once ask any of them to mind me either. I had a mother who was very happy indeed until they came and stuck her in one place, and then stuck me in another place. And even if my mother couldn't mind me for a while, then that was fine too because I could mind myself. I could even mind my mam too, if it came to that. And protect her, if she wanted me to, until she was rested and better. Then we could go back to having her minding me again, and keep taking turns till the end of all time ran out. If these staff people would only let me. We just needed to be allowed to be a family, my mammy and me, like in the old days when we'd be nice and snug by the range in our own kitchen back home. Time to bury my da, who was a jigsaw in the garda station, and then to figure out what we would do next. That's all. But it was too much to ask these know-alls, who hadn't a clue. They didn't even know how little they knew – that's how thick they were.

Conferences went on and on for hours, a bit like prayers and vigils, with non-stop talking, talking, talking, and eating, eating, eating, till either they'd run out of nosey questions to ask and stupid things to say, or till all the cakes were gone. I think that's mostly how they knew when to stop talking. 'We'd better stop now – there's not a single cake left!'

You could tell how important a conference was by the number of cakes the staff bought. If the plates were piled high with cakes and chocolate bars, then it was going to be a very serious one. If there was fresh cream buns, or if one of the staff did baking specially for it, scones and apple tarts and all that, then some really important experts were going to be there for all the staff to show off to. It reminded me of the neighbours at home, when they did all their baking to try and trick me during the siege in our house. I started to get very suspicious of people who did a lot of baking.

Some of the staff went to far too many conferences, because they were huge. I think they had conference disease, if there's such a thing. Only two of them could fit on a bench where four children usually sat for dinner. Some of the fat men experts grew beards to try to look more brainy, and they wore big woolly jumpers that went right up under their chins. Maybe they got a job being Santy at Christmastime when there were no conferences going on, so they could earn extra money for cakes.

I think some of the lady experts used to be teachers, but they got fired from school for being too bossy and for never smiling. Maybe they learned how to smile out of a book, a book with half the pages missing. They hated it when you didn't do things the way they wanted you to. Someone must have told them once that they knew everything – a fortune-teller or someone like that who wanted to keep them happy – and they were so thick they believed it, because they really thought they did know everything. I knew they knew nothing. Egg had been in the home far longer than me, and he told me how it all worked, so I was ready for them.

'That bugs the heads off them, when you're on to all their bollox. First, when you go in they'll be all smiles, and saying your jumper is lovely and all this. Let them shite on a bit. Get a good handful of the bickies first, before you tell them anything.'

'But I don't know what I should tell them, Egg.'

'Tell them to fuck off, like I told ye! Eat the bickies, and then tell them they're all wankers, and to fuck off. That's all. That's not too much to remember, is it, Mucka? Then your part of the conference will be over, and we can play three-and-in out the back. Fair enough?'

'Fair enough, Egg. Oh, by the way, Egg?'

'Yeah?'

'How did you get called Egg?'

'My little brother Gary couldn't say my real name, and he just called me Eggie, and then everyone started, and then that turned into Egg.'

'But what's your real name?'

'Eddie.'

'I think they called you Egg because you're cracked.'

It came to the time for my conference, and I got called into the room. All the staff and experts were smiling at me like I was the baby Jesus or something, just like Egg said. They said a lot of scutter like 'You're getting tall', even though some of them had never even seen me before. Then they asked me would I like a bickie.

'Can I take a few for my friend?' I asked them.

'Of course you can,' they all said at once, and I got a plateful handed to me. They thought things were going well, because they all had a bickie too. But I had my speech ready. One of the fat brain-doctor people, the one with the biggest leather bag, who was probably the boss over them all, asked me if there was anything I would like to say.

'There sure is,' I said, thinking it was a pity Egg couldn't hear all the things I was going to say, because I knew it would have made him very proud of me. I wanted more than anything for him to be proud of me, because he was a good friend to me. I forgot most of what I planned to say when I saw them all staring at me with crumbs in their beards and cream on their chins, and smiling like they were my long-lost aunties and uncles. I forgot all about being calm too, and about my plan to escape without being noticed. I said some of what I'd planned, and other things that just came into my head there and then.

'I'd like to go home now, because you are not my family and I don't want to live here or to be minded by them staff, and especially not by that big red-faced bitch at the end.' By this I meant Hilary, the one who ran the children's home. Egg hated her, and he always called her a red-faced bitch. Mam wouldn't have liked to hear me using that expression, but I couldn't help it. Anyway, I heard my da saying it sometimes at night. I learned a lot of curses in the children's home, and that wasn't the worst of them. Besides which, Hilary *was* a red-faced bitch, so I wasn't telling lies, not like all of them.

That wiped the smiles and the creamy crumbs off their faces. Some of the experts looked at their watches then, and put their pages of writing, which was basically all their rubbish and lies about me, back into their leather bags and cases, along with the last of the Kit Kats. They probably got the lies off the holy rosary neighbours from back home, lies the busy neighbours invented between saying novenas – praying that they would win money, and that their enemies would meet with an accident. The rest of it was probably made up by Uncle Patsy and the red-faced bitch.

Then they all shifted about, like it was time to go suddenly.

'What's the matter – bickies gone already?' I said. 'Or are you wanting to break wind? I wouldn't be surprised, after the feed of tea and bickies you just had.'

I wasn't done yet, even if they were. I said it as loud as I could so Egg could maybe hear what I was saying, if he was outside the door.

'Be sure and put your fat arse out over the half-door before you blow at any rate,' I said, and I suddenly thought of my mother peeling potatoes to beat the band, and it nearly made me cry for a second. I was shouting, and that got them up off their backsides and heading for the door.

There was more blarney then about 'We only want to this and we only want to that and it's all for your own good.' Where had I heard that before?

'My own good! Grand,' I said. 'I'll just get my jacket and you can drop me at the station. If I stay here, I'll only end up being a head case, like all the people who work here, and that would hardly be for my own good, now would it?'

Then Hilary said something about 'our guests' who came all this way to help me, and is this the thanks they get? Egg had told me that they were paid loads of money for working there, and doing conferences every day, so I wasn't going to be taken in by her guff about our poor guests, breaking their hearts to come and see me.

'Don't our guests, as you call them, get all the free cake they can eat? Besides, they're not *my* guests. I never asked for them. Why don't you all go to a conference somewhere else and talk scutter and lies about somebody else, and eat their cakes too, and just fuck off! And you go with them, Hilary, and bring your supply of girls' magazines that you spend all day reading in the staff jacks with the special key so you can hide in there, and nobody will know you're really just examining your spare tyre, instead of working, and bring the supply of chocolate from the reward-press with you. You could never even fit your big elbows into one of those dresses anyway, though you might get a job filling a pothole in the road, by just lying down in it, you overgrown silage heap.'

I had more to say too, but one of the staff took a hold of my arm then, which I did not like one bit, and she should not have done, no way, so I punched her in the face as hard as I could. I was strong for eleven and three-quarters. 'Strong and wiry,' I heard one of the staff say. Suddenly there were three or four of them on top of me, sitting on me and breathing their stinking cake and coffee breath and their snots and farts on me and telling me to calm down.

'How can I calm down with four fat strangers sitting on me and grunting like pigs that weren't fed for three days?'

I was sorry that Egg was missing it all.

Then, in the middle of all the grunting and skitter about being calm, I had the kill feeling. If I had had a knife, I would have cut them all to ribbons. I felt like killing someone, or maybe everyone. Like when the two-day siege ended that time, and I was ready to use the shotgun. They all thought then I wasn't really going to use it, that I only had it to scare them and get them to stop saying the rosary. They thought I didn't even know it was loaded. I knew that I was not being very cunning now, though, and that this was exactly what the adults all wanted me to do – to go ape, as Egg would say, so they could pretend they were doing all this protecting for my own good. So I slowly eased off and calmed down, and gradually I started to be cunning again.

They eventually got off me, slowly, but ready to jump on again if I said 'pigs' or 'fuck' or anything else. I was sore everywhere. The pain of Uncle Patsy's beating came racing back, and a few new pains joined in. The experts were all long gone home for their tea by then. I think Darina, the member of staff I punched, was gone too, because I heard someone saying the home would pay for her taxi to go and get her nose X-rayed. Nobody asked me if I wanted an X-ray. I felt like a half-dozen eggs that someone had dropped.

I decided to stay on the floor for a good while after they all got off me, because I didn't want them to think I was going to get up just when they decided I could. Someone said that they all wanted me to think about my behaviour, and about the pain I had caused to the people who cared for me. Pain? Did my broken bones stick in their arses?

I still felt the kill feeling, listening to the sermon-voice talking about hurting people, but I was getting better at being smart already.

'Wait,' I said in a whisper to myself, 'wait.'

They would never make me do anything, I decided right then. Never. And I would make them pay for every day they kept me from doing what I wanted to do, which was just to go home. That's all I ever wanted.

Hilary was at the kitchen table all the time. I could hear her huffing and wheezing. I could see her fat ankles in her stupid yellow sandals across the floor. She probably thought they were the bee's knees. I was hoping she would have a bad heart attack and join me on the floor. I could just lie there, looking across at her face going purple and black, and her tongue sticking out like a slaughtered sheep's. Or maybe like my da's tongue in that bone tree. And I would not say anything till I was fairly sure the bloated mangy animal was well dead.

Why should she be alive and my da not? She was in charge – she could have told them to let me go – but she wanted to show the experts that she could put manners on me, and show off and get more pay and be put in charge of some bigger care-home prison. But she just sat there, her fat windpipe whistling away like a gale in the bulrushes, and wouldn't die. I started thinking that if I had ugly feet like hers, I'd make sure I wore wellington boots, even in bed. I said the word 'ugly' a few times, but only in a whisper, enough for her to know I was saying something bad, but not enough for her to be able to get me for it. I was too sore to risk having all the pigs kneel their mucky trotters on my back again, telling me how much everyone cared about me.

Ugly. It was like the way my mam used to pray – a whisper.

I hit another staff member the next day. I wasn't planning to hit this one either, but I had to do it. He sounded English, but my da told me before that there were uppity Irish people who really wanted to be English, so maybe he was one of them. Anyway, I forget his name. He was one of the staff I didn't like, so I never remembered his name. He found me trying to escape out of a window and he pulled me back in by the legs. I sat very still while he explained that he was doing it for my own good, and then I forgot all about being cunning again, and when he stopped talking and smiled, I punched him as hard as I could on the nose.

It took him totally by surprise, because he thought his little speech was working, and that I was really listening. He bent down double for a few seconds, and when he sat up straight again his moustache was all thick with blood. It looked like when Da sometimes pulled a chicken's head clean off by accident when he was just trying to break its neck. I told him I knew he was just one of Hilary's little trained monkeys, and then I carried on with my escape because Sir Moustache thought he was doing so well explaining everything to me that he forgot to call for reinforcements. He probably thought he'd get a medal off Hilary if he captured me all on his own. He couldn't really call for help then, because of all the blood coming out of his nose. It was really squirting out, and I had to move away so I wouldn't get it all over me too. He was like a sheep in the abattoir, rolling around and making funny noises. His hair was even kind of white and wavy like a sheep's.

So out I got, and I ran like the rabbits in the fields around my house. I ran even faster than I ran when Uncle Patsy was after me. I promised my lungs and my heart that we'd do something nice when this was all over if they helped me to escape. I heard my name, and sort of looked back to see where it was coming from. Egg opened a window upstairs and shouted after me as I was running.

'Go on, JJ, ye big mad culchie redneck bogtrotter bastard! Leg it, ye big bogger. Run like fuck!'

Fuck would have been proud of me, I ran so fast.

After a couple of miserable nights, they caught me trying to thumb a lift in the wrong direction. In a way I was kind of glad, because I was starving and tired and cold from sleeping under a bridge, and in a ditch. I think I spent most of the first day trying to catch my breath after all the running, and just trying to figure out where I was, and which direction was home. In the end I just went with them, real quietly, to some hostel place for emergency cases, which is what I was. I could never go back to the home, they said, all with real serious faces, like I was going to be crying or something, but I was over the moon to hear that news. Except I probably wouldn't get to see Egg, and one or two staff that had been fairly nice to me in St Somebody's, again. On the way I got a can of Coke, a bag of chips and a hamburger with cheese in it from a social worker. That was the best food I ever had, I was so hungry.

The emergency hostel had locks everywhere, but I was too tired to care. After not much sleep for two nights, and then the big feed of chips, I was starting to fall asleep. The social worker got me checked in, filled in more forms, asked about my mother and my father, all the same as before. Then I went for a pee, and two staff showed me where I would be sleeping. They said they would be awake all night, and if I needed anything, to call them. I don't remember what the room was like – I was too tired to notice where I was. Early the next day they bounced me up before I could even think about trying to run again. It was like jail there anyway. There was another sort of conference thing straight after my cornflakes. It was short, but there was a garda, maybe because I'd hit the staff in the other home.

At least I didn't think they'd brought a garda because I'd wet the bed again. It was the Coke. Mammy would never have allowed that either, and definitely not so late at night.

I didn't hear anything they said after I was brought into their office, which was just a sitting room with a big metal chest of drawers for all the lies to be stored away in. They were probably afraid that they'd forget how many lies they told, or get their lies mixed up if they didn't keep them in neat piles. I think it made them feel more important to call it 'the office'. In that case, the barn back at home was my office. Anyway, they had the same big serious faces as the staff in the first home. They must all have to do some special training in how to make loads of serious faces. And speeches – they all loved their little speeches too.

'Sadly this', and 'unfortunately that', but most of all they all loved when they could say how serious things were.

'We're treating this very seriously, JJ,' they said, with their best big serious faces on.

'I bet you all got an A+ in school for your faces,' I said, but they looked even more serious then.

'Well, being kidnapped and then sat on by smelly fat animals is a very serious thing,' I heard myself say. I wanted them to hear my side too, or if not that, then at least I could let them know that I thought they were all little pigs, rolling in filthy lies. Then I decided not to say any more. I just looked at the floor and thought about my da hiding in the bone tree, and how he wouldn't be coming to get me out of that place. I thought about him stuck between the branches, like a prisoner in a cage made of branches. Maybe he'd been calling for a few days, getting weaker.

'I'm up here, JJ ... up in the tree ... tell someone to get help ... I'm stuck ... good lad ... and JJ? ... tell them to bring a bottle of stout.'

One of the apostles calls me over. He winks at me, and points to the stone above the door of the tomb. Then a few of the apostles help him to push the stone away. They are all smiling and winking, pointing at the little gap into the tomb. They tell me to go in and have a look. I'm not sure what the game is, but since they are the apostles, I squeeze in through the narrow space. It's dark and freezing inside, and I can't see a thing.

I can hear the apostles outside whispering and laughing. I want to go outside and see what they're up to, but the gap is too small when I try to squeeze out. I realise that the apostles are pushing the stone back into place, and I know I'll never move it on my own. They start up the rosary outside. Then I just scream, but the more I scream, the louder the apostles say the rosary.

NINE

THEY MOVED ME TO ANOTHER children's-home prison place that same day. They said it wasn't a prison, but I knew it was. After three weeks in the new 'unit' with no more violence or assaults, and no more being sat on by hippos in tracksuits just for telling them the truth, Fran, the social worker who had me to look after, agreed that I could finally go and visit my mother.

I hadn't seen her since the last day Uncle Patsy had brought me, two weeks before he'd tried to kill me. It was really only a couple of months before, but it felt like it was about ten years. I'd never been apart from my mam for more than a day before all this started, and I couldn't figure out why it had to happen to me and my family. In a way it didn't matter though, because if she was well and I was good, we could just go back to our own house and start all over again.

Uncle Patsy was still my next of kin, as the staff kept reminding me, and he had to sign a form to let me out to see my own mammy. I don't think he wanted to bring me anywhere since I'd got him on the side of the head with wet turf, but he knew Father Nealon would tell him he was a great fella if he took me, so he did. He didn't say much when he came to bring me to the place Mam was in, and neither did I. I was thinking that once I got a chance on my own to explain everything to her, all that had happened, and the mad things that we'd both had done to us, then everything would be alright. Mam would understand why I'd done some of those things then, and she'd know and she'd forgive me straight away, without any more questions, and it would make her better in a second just to hear me explaining it all, and make me feel better too. I knew that it was all very confusing for her, as well as for me.

I decided I wouldn't tell her about Uncle Patsy beating the tar out of me in the field though. He was her brother, after all, and I knew he was cute enough when it came to getting her to like him and think he was a great fella altogether, just like he did with Father Nealon. He did all sorts to try to look like a saint, and poor Mam was so gentle and trusting that she believed the sly old fox. I wasn't going to say another bad word against him, at least not yet. Not till me and her were safe back home and this whole nightmare with my da and the children's home and the hospital and the crows and maggots and fairy sticks and hiding and boxing people and getting sat and farted on and threatened and chased and kicked and brought here there and everywhere was all well and truly behind us.

Then I might tell her that Uncle Patsy was only a bollox. One thing at a time. Be cunning, I kept telling myself, be cunning. Don't let them know what's in your head. Mam and me, we will come out of all this and be alright again. That's what kept me going, thinking that, during all the weeks that I didn't even get to see my own mother.

It was a quiet drive to the convent hospital place where Mammy was resting. She must be the best-rested person in Ireland by now, I thought, but I didn't say that to Uncle

Patsy. He'd only have grunted at me and told me not to be a smart fella, or he'd have to burst me again in another field. He more or less said that anyway, just as we arrived at the convent.

'No monkey business, me buck,' he said.

Then he let me see that he had a hurley under an old coat on the back seat of the van. He didn't say anything, just let me see it. Patsy would love to finish me off, I knew that, and leave Mammy to be minded by the nuns for good. Then he could get his greedy little hands on our farm, and have the place all to himself. That would suit him grand. I think that's all he ever wanted. He was really secretly delighted when poor Da went missing.

He could just say that I made him crash the van or something, or better still, that I stole it and crashed it trying to escape. Then he'd roll it down Piggery Hill some night with my battered corpse in the driver's seat, and by the time it hit Reilly's wall in the bend, it would be up to a fair speed. It might even go on through the wall and into the lake. Who would doubt him? He was always up in the front row at Mass, touching his breast with the very hand that had welted me, and talking to Father Nealon outside, and tut-tutting about this and that bad thing, the weather or people who drank too much and gambled, though I saw a quare lot of bottles around his house, and the old newspapers were all open on the racing page.

His old van was a rusty pile of sheep-stinking old shite anyway, and he probably thought he would get a new one when he'd have our farm. You could hardly see out the windscreen for all the flies buzzing on the inside, and moths squashed to bits on the outside. Except he wasn't going to have our farm, because JJ was getting wise too, as sly as a fox, and well up to them all and all their antics.

I got a bit of a shock when I saw Mammy. It was more like it really was ten years since I'd seen her. For someone who'd been catching up on her sleep for weeks on end, she looked awful tired, with dark bags under her eyes. She didn't even get up out of the big old armchair when we came in. I thought maybe the nuns had glued her into it. Her hair was grey all of a sudden too, like Da's was before. She had some old woman's dress and cardigan on her too, not her own clothes, and they were too big for her. I didn't recognise anything she had on, except the scarf with the horses on it, which was tied loose around her shoulders. I kissed her cheek, and she sort of smiled, but not as big a smile as I would have liked, and she didn't try to hug me, like I'd been imagining and dreaming about for ages. There was a smell from somewhere too, like my old sheets. Maybe the fairies just gave up trying to kidnap Mam and settled for putting a sleeping spell on her instead.

There was a nun like a big circus tent in the corner near the window, blocking out all the light. Uncle Patsy came and put his hand on my mother's arm for a second, and then went over and whispered with the nun for a while. I decided to wait till they were gone before I'd tell Mammy all that was after happening. Patsy left after a while, but the big nun stayed in the room. So I decided I'd just do what they did. I just whispered to Mammy. Even though she looked so strange, I was sure that once she got out of those dead clothes and had her hair curled up, and heard all my news, and my plans, although I hadn't made them fully yet, I was certain that she would start to feel better right away.

I kneeled down in front of her, like I used to do at home in our kitchen in front of the range on cold wet days like this one. I noticed her rosary beads and little purse, and some novenas on her lap. There were new novenas too. I looked at some of them. I thought I knew every saint on the planet, but there were a few more saints I'd never heard of in her big bundle of prayers.

'Did the Bishop make up some more saints since?' I asked.

She didn't answer. She just dabbed her eye with a hanky, and I noticed that her hand was a little bit shaky, like Da's hands used to be in the mornings.

'I'm sorry about before,' I said then. 'You know, what happened at the house. I was just protecting you, us, from ... things.' Mam dabbed her eyes with the hanky again, and made a kind of a noise like a small frightened bird, and then the nun rustled over nearer, like she wanted to hear our private conversation. I wanted to tell her to go and darn the priest's long johns, and mind her own business, when I remembered Uncle Patsy's hurley.

I thought of asking her if she was teaching my mother how to do bird impressions, but decided not to say anything that could possibly upset anyone. I could see Patsy outside the window now that the nun was no longer blocking the view. He was smoking a cigarette and leaning on his skittery van. I could tell he was itching to use that hurley.

'I think my mother is very thrilled to see me,' I said up to the shadow above me, as nicely as I could, and without grinding my teeth.

'You're a very lucky boy,' the big nun said.

She had me there, because I had no clue how I was lucky exactly, but I just held Mam's hand and said up to the big Shadow Mother that I knew I was lucky.

Lucky that I figured out how to outfox a whole town full of slippery eels.

I just wanted her to go back to counting her beads or her money or whatever she was at. She stood there though, looking at me and then looking at Mam, back and forth, like she was trying to decide which of us she would eat first.

I felt tears then in my own eyes, and I was furious, because I didn't want them there, not in front of the big tent of a nun especially. I had a sudden picture in my head of just running at her and pushing her with my head in her big gut across the room and straight through the big window. She might even land on Uncle Patsy and kill them both. We'd see then what Uncle Patsy, the Patron Saint of Thieves and Liars, would think about having a bloated pig sitting on his face, like I had to put up with in the home he'd put me into. But that would be the end of going home with my mother and starting over again, so I just let the nun see my tears. I hoped she would leave us be if she saw how upset me and my mother were about everything that had happened, and about my da being a jigsaw above in the barracks, and his bones not even buried yet because they were still in a cell, where the Sergeant was adding new bones whenever Spinner ran in with one, wagging his tail. When the jigsaw was all finished and Mammy was rested enough, then we could have a proper funeral.

She stood there for another while, staring. Then she said I was a lucky boy again, and said I'd have to leave my mam to have her rest very soon, and she rustled off towards her money-rosary. Before she sat down, she pointed a finger at me and told me not to say anything to upset my poor mother. I had never upset my poor mother all my life. I was always trying to help her, every day, and now here was another red-faced fat bitch who knew nothing about my family butting in and interfering and making up more lies. And why was my mam not well rested by now if this Big Top of a nun was caring for her so well? Was this nun keeping her here by giving her medicine to make her sleep?

Maybe Uncle Patsy and Mother Big Top were in cahoots to get our farm between them, by keeping Mammy half-asleep for ever, and me in the prison for children who are too clever for the liking of lying adults.

Suddenly Mam was looking into my face with a very worried look, like she knew I was thinking something bad. I knew I had to stop, so I made myself smile then and say that I was grand and that she looked grand too.

'I like the place I'm living in, Mammy, I really do. The staff there look after us fierce well, and the other children are all very friendly. We go swimming every week to a big swimming pool near us, and we might be going to the pictures, too. And we say the rosary and go to Mass in Irish and everything. At least the priest comes in and says Mass for the whole place. I bet you'd love it, Mam!'

I said a few more things like that, loud enough for Mother of All Sorrows to hear me, and for a minute I even started to think maybe the place I was living in wasn't so bad. Mam looked a bit more calm then too, and she put her arm around my neck and gave me the first hug I'd had off her in I don't know how long. That nearly got me crying again, but I held back the tears, because if I cried any more then Mammy would start too, and the big Mother who was nobody's mother would say right, that's it, away out with you.

I knew now was not the time to tell Mammy everything. In fact I knew going out the door of that convent-place that I might never be able to tell her absolutely everything, because things were not the way I'd expected them to be. This needed some crafty thinking, more than ever before. It was a good job I'd started to practise being cunning before all this happened, because I was sure going to need all I could get from now on.

I was quiet all the way back to the home after my visit, trying to work it all out.

If only I could have gone to one of my hideouts on our own farm. If I could only have been back there for an hour or two, I'd have had it all sorted out in jig-time.

I'm up at the old house where my mother was born. The stairs are all rotten, but I've made it to the top by keeping to the sides. Mam's mother and father are asleep in the big old iron bed. There's a crooked crucifix on the wall. It's rusted from rain getting in. Under where slates are missing, thick grey webs hang with damp, like bad phlegm when you're sick.

My mam is cuddled up between her parents in the bed. Swallows come in and out of the broken windows, but they don't seem to bother anyone in the bed. Mam gets up to pray to the cross. The blanket comes away and the springs of the old iron bed are full of bones. Small ones fall through the springs on to what's left of the floor; some even tumble down into the old parlour below. Bigger bones get stuck in the springs and vibrate gently there, as if they'd like to be alive again. Skulls are where the pillows should be. Mammy takes down the rusty cross and starts to pray hard.

'Jesus protect us from holes in the ground and coffins and cold clay. Most of all protect us from the worms. Amen.'

'But Mam,' I say, 'Jesus knows everything before we even say it, so He knows all that anyway. That's what you always say.'

Jesus the big know-all, I say, but under my breath.

Then Mam goes out a door, like she's heard me. I follow her. The floorboards are all rotten away on the other side of the door, but somehow she's gone.

TEN

THE STAFF COULDN'T GET OVER IT. I became the best-behaved boy they ever had living in that place for not-very-well-behaved boys. I even made friends with other children in the home, and played with everyone and did my work and never argued or cursed or anything. I went to bed and got up again when I was told. I went to school and worked hard to catch up with all the stuff I'd missed since September. I ate every dinner the staff cooked, and never said I don't like this, or that's crap, like some of the children did. I made my bed and kept my room tidy, and did any jobs the staff gave me to do. Sometimes I even offered to do extra.

Once when my social worker, Fran, phoned up to see how I was, I heard the staff saying to him that he must have brought back the wrong boy the last time, I was so changed and polite and good. They said it was hard to believe that I'd once assaulted two staff. The next time Fran came, which was not to visit me, but to bring in another boy to live in the home, he told the staff they were doing a great job. I knew I hadn't changed, though. I was still the same me I always was – just none of these strangers ever knew me in the first place.

There were two boys in the home who were about my own age, and I started to play football and pal around with them. They were both from Dublin too, but they didn't know Egg. They came from different parts of the city, flats that sounded horrible, with no grass or anywhere to play or walk or hide, and burning cars and broken glass everywhere. It sounded like some other country where there was a war going on.

We all had nicknames for each other. I was always just called Mucka, because I was from a farm. I thought it was a bit silly, but it made the other two laugh and I didn't really mind, so the name kind of followed me. One lad said he was always just called Spider, because he was good at climbing over walls and robbing orchards, and the other was nicknamed Gickna, because in the flats he was from he kept pigeons, and in Dublin they called pigeons gicknas, or at least that was what they called the ones that were no good. I didn't know why anyone would want to rob an orchard, or to keep pigeons as pets, and I was shocked when I heard that you had to pay for the pigeons. Pigeons were a pest where I came from, and people shot them, and ate them too, if there wasn't too many shotgun pellets in them. Spider said he'd seen Gickna's pigeons, and that they should be shot. He said that they were all lame and had hard dry bits of shit in their toes, and one eye gone and feathers missing all over, and fleas, which is what a real gickna is. Gickna didn't seem to mind Spider saying all that about his precious pigeons. He'd just wait till Spider was finished and then say, 'Yeah, Spider, scabby and covered in shite, like your aul one.'

Then we'd all laugh our heads off. That was Gickna's answer whenever anyone said anything bad to him – 'Yeah, like your aul one.' They never said 'my mam', like I did, just 'your aul one'. I liked the way Spider and Gickna talked. It reminded me of Egg, and I often wondered how he was getting on. Maybe if Egg punched one of the staff in the nose, he might get moved up to live with Spider and Gickna and me. I decided to ask the staff for the proper name and address of St Somebody's, and write a letter to Egg and tell him my plan to get us all together in the same place. I could even suggest which staff to punch.

Their accents were funny, and the things they came out with sometimes had me laughing till my sides were sore. They thought my country accent was funny too, and the way I pronounced some words made them cry laughing, like I never saw people laughing before. They'd say the word over and over to each other, and then ask me to say it again, and that would start them off, till I'd get bored waiting for them to get tired out. Or I'd be just kind of carried along by them, and end up holding my ribs too.

'What the fuck are you laughin' for, ye big bog man? You bleedin' said it in the first place! The big red neck on ye!'

Then they'd be off again. I'd try to copy the way they'd say 'bleedin', and that would leave the three of us weak from laughing. That was another thing – they cursed all day long, even worse than Egg. I asked them if their mams or dads minded them cursing.

'Sure who the fuck do ye think taught us how to curse, ye big bogger?' they said, and laughed again. Apart from Egg, Spider and Gickna were the first friends I ever had. Spinner was my friend too, but he was a dog. Spider and Gickna said they thought I was alright too, for a bog man.

Once Spider and Gickna asked me about my family, and I said my da was in a prison for skeletons, and my mother was a melting snowman.

'Ye know wha', Mucka, you're bleedin' stone mad you are.'

Then I said I wouldn't be surprised if I was. 'My mother is definitely mad,' I said.

We all laughed, but I was sorry straight away that I'd said it, and I wanted to see Mam there and then and tell her I didn't mean it. Even when people aren't with you, you can hurt them.

That's how things went, school and homework and then playing and messing with Spider and Gickna, and other boys sometimes, till my first ever Christmas away from home was just around the corner. The Christmas before that was my first one ever without my da, and I thought that was as bad as my life could be, till maybe there'd be a big war or something. A big war might have been better. At least it might have got rid of a few of your enemies for you, do you a favour, and then you couldn't be blamed for starting the war that got them all killed off.

I had a few phone calls from my mam, but there was always someone listening in, and the calls were too short. I could never say anything I wanted to say, and then sometimes I didn't really know any more what it was I'd really wanted to say in the first place. After a couple of minutes, Mammy would start yawning or crying or being a frightened bird again, and saying she was very tired and that she had to go. I wanted to ask her how the fuck she could still be tired after being in bed for five or six months, but I remembered that the Mother of All Sorrows was probably listening in on the other end too, and would run across the fields flattening all the thistles with her big barge feet to tell Uncle Patsy if I said one wrong thing.

I only wanted to know when Mam would finally be finished with all her rest, and how soon we could go home together. I even told Spider and Gickna that they could come and visit me when I was back on our farm – maybe soon, like just for Christmas maybe, which is what I was planning. They both said they wouldn't be caught dead on a farm, but then they said it sounded like it would be a good laugh. Anywhere Spider and Gickna went was bound to be a good laugh, even if they went into a graveyard at night with no flash lamp.

One day I asked Mo, one of the staff who was mostly fair to me, if I could have the address for Egg, and if I could ring my mother. I also said I wanted to ring Fran, who hadn't been near me or called me for months. Spider said the best way to see your social worker was to smash a window, or try to run away, but I didn't want to give them an excuse to tell me I couldn't go home.

'Well, well,' Mo said. 'You've been busy making plans, haven't you?'

'I'd really like to see about going home at Christmas.'

Mo said she'd find out for me. A couple of days after that she called me into a room with dolphins on the walls and lamps with oil moving around in them and music on, except it wasn't music really, it was like waves in the sea. There was even the noise of seagulls on the tape, which sounded a bit mad in that tiny room. I'd never seen the sea, but I didn't tell anyone that. Fran was there too, even though I didn't phone him, and the lamp reflecting on his face made him look like he was swimming with the dolphins. I started to laugh when I saw him – a dolphin with glasses and a briefcase. I was thinking what a howl Spider and Gickna would have when they heard about this. Maybe I was a bit nervous, especially when I saw through the waves that Fran had his best serious social worker face on, his A+ grade one. The staff called this the quiet room, but all the other children said it was the Bad News room.

Somebody must have decided that when you get bad news, the best way to hear it is listening to a fake tape of seagulls and waves with dolphins floating around. And you have to sit on a beanbag, because the Bad News room was the only place in the home that had beanbags. There was one big armchair jammed into the corner for overgrown staff who were afraid to sit on a beanbag, because then they couldn't get up without help. Spider told me that a very fat staff member called Dinny had got beaten up by a boy the year before, because Dinny made the mistake of sitting on the beanbag while he was telling this boy some bad news. The boy jumped on Dinny and started welting hell out of him, and Dinny couldn't get out of the beanbag to defend himself. So that's when they put in the armchair for the fat staff.

'Now, JJ, are you nice and comfy?' Mo smiled a B- smile, and looked at Fran to see how he would react. Fran did a B- smile back.

'Do you like beanbags, JJ?' Mo asked. 'Try one, they're fun.'

Mo was in the armchair, though she probably could still have managed a beanbag, so there wasn't really anywhere else for me to sit.

'Now, since our little chat the other day, I've spoken to Fran about what might happen for you at Christmas. Fran called Sister Noleen at the convent and had a talk about how your mother is getting along. Your Uncle Patsy said he was very keen that – '

'And?'

I had to ask her because Mo didn't seem to think I was interested in finding out exactly how my mother was getting along.

'Pardon?' Mo had on her A+ grade confused face.

'How is my mother getting along? Has she woken up yet?'

I knew I shouldn't say stuff like that, but I was finding it very difficult to be crafty just at that particular time. I wanted to hear that there was great news, that my mother was back to her old self, more or less, and that I could go home as soon as my bag was packed. I wanted to turn off the stupid seagulls, and the grinning dolphins, and the oily thing going round and round on the walls, and arrange my leaving-this-pigsty party. But it wasn't looking good. Good news you can tell fast; bad news takes a long time to get to, and Mo was taking a long time.

Fran the dolphin social worker chipped in. 'She is really doing very, very well, JJ, and getting the best care you could wish for her. Sister Noleen and your Uncle Patsy are seeing to that.'

'I bet they are. Sister Scrooge and her pet snake,' I heard myself saying, before I could stop it coming out. Mo and Fran were silent then for a bit, trying to figure out if they'd heard me right, I suppose. I was working it out myself, to be sure that's what I'd really said. Fran rustled some papers then and carried on.

'The fact is, JJ, that your mother is not quite ready to face up to the stress of Christmas, and she feels – '

'Who says she's not quite ready? You? Uncle Patsy? Scrooge? Who? And what stress are you talking about? It's just me and my mam eating a roast chicken, that's all.'

Suddenly I could feel all my cunning slipping around the walls with the oily lamp.

Mo decided it was her turn to have a go again. That's how they mostly did things in the home: one has a try, then when that doesn't work the other butts in, and so on, like the vet and my da taking turns trying to inject a lively heifer.

'JJ, we have to make the best decision for everyone here. I know how much you'd love to get home for Christmas, but it wouldn't be very fair if we tried to make your mum go home when she doesn't really feel up to it yet, now would it? That might upset her all over again, and you wouldn't want to do that to your mother, now would you, JJ? Not after all she's been through already.'

I looked at my runners, and shook my head, and for the first time in a long time I got the kill feeling, but stronger and worse than ever before. It nearly came right out and did something bad, there and then in the quiet room, in front of all the peaceful dolphins and squawking gulls and gentle false waves. But I got one last drop of cunning from an emergency supply that I keep in a quiet part of my brain, a part of my brain that was sort of like a hideout that I didn't use very often, and I managed to stay on the beanbag. Maybe that's what the beanbags were for – to give you a few extra seconds to think. Fran and Mo kept talking for another while, but I didn't hear anything they were saying. They sounded very calm and dead impressed with each other at how they'd got this boy to listen to all their gibberish, guff and scutter, and neither of them realised how they could easily have had their throats cut with sharp bits of a smashed stupid oily dolphin-lamp.

Uncle Patsy must have been looking for another pat on the back from Father Nealon, because he finally said he would bring me to his house, if I wanted to go, and if I promised to behave, on Christmas Day. Behave? As if I'd really want a hurley broken across my back, which is what Patsy would give me for Christmas if he had half a chance. I knew he only offered to do it to make himself look good to all the staff, and Father Nealon and Sister Ferret Face would think he was a great lad. I didn't care though. I decided it was time to get away from the home and think what the hell I was going to do next. I wasn't going to stay there for ever while all the adults decided what was best for me. One dose of the dolphin treatment was enough for me.

Uncle Patsy said he would collect me early on Christmas morning, bring me to Mass, then to his house for dinner, and back to the home after teatime. There would be no going to see our old farm or our house. Fran and Patsy and Mo and Sister Ferret had all decided it might only 'upset' me. They didn't seem to think that being locked up in a hole with big sows sniffing around after me all day and night might be upsetting me even more. The home said they would bring me to see my mother on Christmas Eve, but not for too long a visit, because she found Christmas a very 'emotional' time, Mo said.

That was the deal. That, or stay in the home for Christmas.

ELEVEN

THERE WAS NOWHERE TO HIDE IN the home. The staff had thought of everything, so no child could be out of sight for more than about three seconds. They'd even want to know what was keeping you if you were too long in the toilet. I needed to do some serious thinking, and get things clear in my head without Mo, or any of the rest of the staff, or Fran or Spider and Gickna talking and laughing and distracting me. So two days after my meeting with Mo and Fran, I said I was feeling sick, and they said all right, I could stay in bed because I'd never been sick in the home before.

Bed is not the best hiding place I ever had, not by a long shot, but it had to do for now. Under the blankets was dark and quiet, and when I closed my eyes and concentrated hard, I could pretend I was back in the barn at home, waiting for Mammy to call me in for my tea. I'd pretend Da was just up in the town, delayed on some business, and he'd be in good form when he'd get back. Mam would send him to look for me, when tea was ready.

'Where's that slippery wee gossoon of a fella now, I wonder?' I'd hear his big loud voice booming across the yard, scattering the chickens, and then I'd crouch down good and tight because I'd know he was on for looking for me.

One thing I knew before I'd even started to think about it: I was not staying in prison for Christmas. If Mammy was not ready or rested or whatever enough to come back home, well I sure was ready. If I could get back to our old house and have the place all straightened out and cleaned up like Mam used to like it, maybe then she'd see that it wasn't so impossible to think about living back there again, even without Da. I knew they would not all just let me go, though. I knew that I'd have to plan my escape, and then make sure that I was not caught standing out in the middle of the road again with my thumb in the air like a big eejit.

I couldn't tell anyone, not even Gickna and Spider, what I was thinking of doing. Not that I didn't trust them, but you'd just never know how the staff might get wind of something, and then maybe start to blackmail other children, or bribe them, to blurt out what they knew. Offer them extra sweets, or to watch the late film on telly or something. Or else get no sweets and no telly if they didn't tell. That's usually how they did it.

Uncle Patsy was going to be a problem – maybe the biggest problem – in my escape plans. He'd stay up all night to find me and kill me with his hurley and his big fists. He probably thought our house was as good as his by now, and the sight of me standing in the hall door with my arm around my mam would drive him out of his mind with rage, I was sure of that. Lying there in the dark under my blankets, pretending to be sick and dreaming of being back in the barn in my old house, I knew something might have to happen to stop Patsy from getting me, before I could persuade Mam that it was all grand to come home and start again. I wasn't sure what that thing would be yet, but I had it now on my list of plans for fixing how things had all gone wrong. Mo always said that that's how you start to make changes to things you don't like – you put them down on your change-list.

'Once the question is planted there in your head, you'll find that an answer soon starts to follow it,' she said.

As far as I could see, the staff mostly didn't care if you got away somehow, or absconded, as they called it. When another boy ran away during a trip to the picture-house for his birthday, I heard them talking about it, and all they were worried about was that they might get in trouble for not keeping a better eye on the boy. The staff called the gardaí and the gardaí had to put down their tea and go out in the cold to look for the missing boy.

Who else might be a problem? Sister Ferret Face I could just push out the window, like I'd planned to before. She'd be no use without Uncle Patsy to protect her, and probably wouldn't mind once I told her I wasn't going to take any of her money, just my mother. Her money would be no good to me anyhow, because if I turned up in a shop anywhere for miles around, they'd catch me. I'd seen films on telly like that before, where the little old man and woman who run the shop give each other a look when a runaway or a convict comes in. Then one carries on smiling and chatting all about how grand the weather is, while the other slips off like an eel and telephones the cops, and the sly old couple get the reward.

I figured I'd have to be like the rabbits back on our farm more than ever, if I was to really stand a chance of not being caught, at least till Mam was back to her old self and able to protect me again. It wasn't the best time of year either to be trying to live in fields and ditches and burrows, right in the middle of winter, but I couldn't stand waiting until spring to escape from the place. At least I knew where my mother was. What would happen if they decided to move her and not tell me – how would I ever find her then? Da was still in the police station, waiting to rest in peace.

So I made up my mind to run for it, and the best time to go would be on a trip out of the home. The only thing was, the way things were looking, that just might have to be on Christmas Day with Uncle Patsy. That was the only outside trip coming up.

I'm walking up the drive to our house with three trout I've caught in the Weal. They're all a good size and I'm dying to show them to Da, and then Mammy can cook them for tea. The door is shut. When I knock, Hilary answers. I try to get past her but she blocks the whole door. I go around to the back but Darina is at the back door, very cross-looking and with a black eye.

I can see Mammy inside at the table with people I don't know, all sitting around, talking. There is a staff member at every window in the house. I start throwing stones at the windows, breaking them and calling my mam to please come out. The people inside won't let her, and they are telling her lies about me, and eating all the cakes the neighbours made.

I find a pitchfork at the back of the house and stick it into Hilary. Then staff come running from every direction, and I run back down the drive, cut across a field, and head for one of my hideouts. I rub muck, dock leaves and nettles on my hands to get off the bad blood.

TWELVE

UNCLE PATSY'S FACE WAS LIKE A flypaper hanging from the peak of the filthy cap he always wore, even on Christmas morning. He didn't get out of his filthy jalopy when he arrived to collect me, because it was sleeting, and there was so much pig slurry, cow-dung and black muck stuck to the windows, I wasn't sure if there was anyone in the van at all, not till I opened the door and sat into the passenger seat. It was hard even then to make out Uncle Patsy, for all the cigarette smoke. The smell in the van made me feel sick, and I nearly cried and ran back into the home, but I had my mind made up to escape, so I sat still and waited for him to set off towards Piggery Hill.

Uncle Patsy didn't speak a word. He drove slowly at first, because the road was getting bad with the sleet, but went faster as he got nearer home. When we hit the top of Piggery Hill, I pretended the space under his legs was a burrow, and that I had three seconds to get down there, or a fox would get me. Then I just made a sort of blind headfirst dive. Piggery Hill is one steep hill, all the way down to the lake, and I knew this would be the best place if my plan had any hope of working.

I jammed myself into the small space at his feet before he knew what was happening. I went in under his legs, squashed myself well in, and he couldn't kick me or hit me because I was stuck in so tight. Anyway, he was too shocked and surprised, and he was driving and trying really hard to keep from skidding and crashing. He took his foot off the accelerator, but I kept pushing the pedal back down with my hand. Then I wriggled onto my side, reached up between his knees and pulled the steering wheel any way I could.

You could roll any car down that hill without accelerating at all, just with the brake off, and still get a right good speed up by the time you hit the bottom, at Reilly's wall. The sleet was making it all the better for me. I even said a quick thank you to God for sending a big shower of sleet as my Christmas present.

Patsy was swearing in a way that would have shocked his best old pal, the Mother of All Sorrows, and he was stamping his feet like crazy trying to stop the van. By then I had stuck the little holy water font that Mammy had given me on my Christmas Eve visit to her the day before under the brake, and the brake wouldn't go down. It was the first time in my life that I ever believed in holy water. Uncle Patsy tried to pull up the handbrake, and I couldn't have stopped him, but I'd put my winter coat over the handbrake when I got into the van, so he couldn't get a proper lift on it. The handbrake didn't really work properly anyway, because the van was such a heap. It actually came right off in Uncle Patsy's hand once, and he welded it back on himself because he was too mean to pay a garage to do it.

I pushed the accelerator to the floor again while he struggled with my coat and the handbrake, and the van skidded, and screeched like a wild animal in a snare. I heard him saying, 'Oh Jesus, Jesus Christ,' like the climbing garda in the big pine tree, and I knew then that we were going to come to a sharp halt soon, one way or the other. I curled as tight as a hedgehog under Uncle Patsy's legs. I think I even held his legs, and then there was a terrible crash and the noise of metal being scraped and bent. Then we were turning over and over and bumping and bashing. Patsy's legs were still kicking, or trembling, when the van finally stopped.

I opened my eyes. All I could see was withered rushes and water, and the water was getting red where it came in at the window near Uncle Patsy's head.

I had to crawl back out the way I'd got in, but it was hard because I was sore, and the van was more on its side, the driver's side. I was crawling arse-first backwards to get out the passenger window. There was a lot of water splashing in at the door, Patsy's door, in front of my face, like water in the bottom of a boat on the lake when Da and me went fishing. I still didn't know where all the blood was coming from, or if Uncle Patsy was alive or dead. I was half-expecting to get a wallop on the side of the head as soon as I was out from under his feet.

I thought I'd better take the hurley from the back of the van, if it was still there, and get it out the window somehow, just in case he was going to be sitting there on a big rock on the shore in a blind rage, waiting for me. The water was coming up to my face, though, and I had to struggle extra fast the last bit of the way, and hold the back of the seat on my side to pull myself away fully. The van shifted a bit, like it was balanced on a ledge, but ready to head for deep water.

Then I saw Uncle Patsy for the first time. He was already nearly covered in water, red water, and his teeth were lost somewhere, and his long bit of grey hair was like sheep's wool in a puddle, only it was on a big scalp of flesh that wasn't attached to his head any more. More thick red was swirling from his middle, thick like the red paint Da used once on the gates to get rid of the rust, or the red raddle he put on some of the sheep, to show they were married. Part of the steering wheel seemed to be in Uncle Patsy's middle somewhere. I knew then that I could leave the hurley where it was. I twisted myself slowly around, so my face was up against my own door again, and I pushed hard a few times. It was bent, though, and wouldn't budge. The water was pouring into the van now, and it was shifting again from me moving in it, so there was no time to fiddle around.

The window was half-smashed, so I started to climb through that. I had to stand on Uncle Patsy's head a bit to hoosh myself up and crawl out. I didn't like the feeling of my feet against his head, moving like a slippery wet rock under me. We were in around withered old rushes, not too far into the lake, but it got deep rapidly near the shore, and the van just suddenly went right under with a sort of fart noise. I was far enough out through the broken window to make a grab for the thick clumps of withered rushes in the shallows, and I kicked. It was so cold, I thought I'd never get out of the lake alive.

The van did more farts, and while it was going down it sucked at me like a sinking ship, but I thought of Patsy's body full of eels peeping out to see who else was coming, and I thought of Da up that tree whispering for water with stringy brown spit in his mouth, and of Mammy in a pissy old convent, and that made me kick harder and I felt some ground under my feet after a few seconds and I just threw myself forward onto the stones in the shallow water.

There was a big track in the old rushes where the van had burst through and rolled in. Phil Reilly's wall was half-wrecked. I was shivering so much, I could hardly walk. My skin was blue, and I could see red streaks trickling from cuts I had got from the broken glass now I was out of the water, but the main thing was there was no guts coming out of my middle like Uncle Patsy had, and there was nobody else around. Nobody had seen or heard us coming down Piggery Hill. The Reillys were in the town, along with all the other neighbours, at Mass for Christmas morning. So they would discover the hole in the wall coming back from Mass, and then a big search would start. I knew I had to get away from there before anyone turned up. For once I was grateful to Father Nealon for the big codology of a sermon that would keep everyone at the church for as long as possible, till I'd get to blazes away.

Of course I could always just hand myself over, and say it was a terrible accident, but then I would only be brought back to the home, so where was the use in being found? This time I was going to hide better than anyone had ever hidden before, even the rabbits. This time I would never be found, not unless I wanted to be. And now Uncle Patsy was out of the way, our farm was safe, and Mammy and me could go back there when we had a few more things sorted out. I would be twelve soon, and we'd be well able to manage. I took one look back at the lake before I headed for cover.

'Happy Christmas, Uncle Patsy,' I said half out loud through my chattering teeth. 'If they have it in Hell.'

THIRTEEN

THERE WAS A RUINED OLD CASTLE on one side of the lake. People always said it was haunted, and that you could hear a man dragging chains around in the big old dining hall there at midnight. I think that was mostly to scare children and keep us from going to play in the castle. Up until then the ghost story had worked, but this was an emergency. It was all covered in ivy and briars, and there wasn't any roof. That was the first place I headed for after Uncle Patsy went into the lake in his submarine.

I kept in close to the ditches on the way, and walked on stones whenever I could, so as not to leave any tracks. Sometimes I walked in the mucky parts where the cows' hooves left deep tracks, so there'd be no human footprints. I took big handfuls of hay from a galvanised iron cattle feeder where it kept dry, and stuffed hay into my wet clothes, up the front of my jumper and down the back, and into my trousers, and up the legs of my trousers. I even stuffed some hay up my sleeves. The cows looked at me, probably wondering why I wasn't eating the hay like everyone else. But it helped me to stop shivering and bleeding, and it gave me camouflage too, like the Irish rebels always had when they were practising to chase out the English.

I wondered what I looked like. Maybe I could be a human scarecrow, I thought, and just stand still whenever anybody was passing by. Then I wouldn't have to stay hiding all the time. I could come out and get food, and find out what was going on, before slipping back into the shadows again. I could just take a spot in the field near the convent where my mam was. Nobody would know who had put up the scarecrow, and they'd all think it was a brilliant idea. I'd make sure no crows ever got so much as a grain of wheat or barley, and I'd have a job for life. Even if someone did discover the truth about me being an actual human later on, by then I'd have made such a good impression with scaring the crows that they'd want to keep me for good anyway. Then I could at least see Mammy every day, at the window, or if she came to sit outside on sunny days. She'd see me there, but she wouldn't know why I looked familiar.

'That scarecrow ... I don't know what it is, something that reminds me ... ah, I don't know. Imagine me thinking a scarecrow can be like a real person. I'd better go in and lie down.'

'You do that, Mam. You just lie down, and when you've had enough sleep in ten or twenty years, I'll be right here waiting to get you home!'

'JJ is the quare one for hiding, all right,' she'd say. 'Like father, like son.'

That's how I made my way to the castle. There was a crumbled part of a wall where the animals used to shelter from bad weather, and a few cows just quietly lying there frightened the life out of me. For a second I thought that somehow Uncle Patsy had escaped from the van and got to the castle first. The cows stopped chewing the cud and stared, clouds of steam coming out of their big nostrils, the frost on the grass all melted around their big warm scutter-brown bodies. I said sook-sook-sook a few times, to let them know I wasn't there to kick their arses, and then I crawled slowly into the thickest part of the briars, right in the middle of the ruins.

I was too cold to feel any pain from the thorns, and my hay suit protected me. I pulled my jumper over my head, and just kept crawling and pushing right through the middle of it all. I started to think of a story I liked at school, when I was small, called 'Brer Rabbit'. When Fox caught him stealing, Brer Rabbit begged Fox not to throw him into the thorny briar patch. Brer Rabbit was crafty, and he knew that if he begged Fox not to do it, then that's exactly where Fox would throw him. Which Fox did, and Brer Rabbit skipped off laughing down his burrow in the middle of the briars, where Fox couldn't follow him. Brer Rabbit was as cheeky as a magpie.

At the very back wall of the castle there was the opening of an old chimney. It was big enough for me to sit inside once I'd kicked and pushed enough thorns and branches out of my way. I couldn't see up the chimney because it was blocked with more branches, and spiders' webs like the big dirty nylon curtains in Uncle Patsy's kitchen, and more briars. I pulled down a lot of stuff that was blocking the chimney, and then when I'd pushed that all out, more sticks came down from old jackdaws' nests, sticks and twigs and leaves and dirt and dust from hundreds of years ago.

There was part of a skeleton of something, something small, in the middle of it all, and it made me think of my da for a few seconds, but I didn't have time to feel sorry because I was too busy making the best hideout of my entire life. The dirt started to fill up the chimney grate again, and I often had to stop myself from sneezing, which would have been a dead giveaway to anyone out hunting for me. Or, the cows could get a fright if I took a fit of coughing, and run off down the hill. Then someone might decide to come up and see what had set them off. After an hour pulling stuff down on top of myself to make more room, there was jelly like Mammy's semolina pudding coming down my nose. I pulled roots and twigs down, then dumped it out, the way I'd come in, then I pulled more down, and dumped that out too. It really was like a rabbit digging a burrow, except I was digging a burrow up and not down.

After a while, the inside of the chimney was like Brer Rabbit's parlour. It got a bit warmer too, and I stopped shivering as much. It was only little shivers, with breaks in between. I lay there then, in my beginning of a burrow in the sky, thinking about what had happened.

Uncle Patsy was as dead as a turkey cock, I knew that much. Would they think I was dead too, at the deep bottom of the lake, when they discovered his body but not mine? That would be the best thing. Then they wouldn't be searching the countryside for an escaped murderer child.

'The child is believed to be disguised as a scarecrow, and may be living up a chimney. This would be no surprise, because his late father was known to like being up trees. Approach with caution. A number of staff in children's homes where he lived briefly were put out of action by his swift left hook . And now for the weather forecast.'

They used to say there was a pike that had swallowed a dog whole in that lake, a dog called Rusty that belonged to a man called Gorman on the far side of the lake. A pike with a huge fat white belly on it like the men in the pubs in town have. When people didn't catch any trout in the lake, they'd say it was that hungry devil of a pike that was gulping his fill of all the best trout in the place. Some people said he ate a few lambs too, lambs that got too frisky buck-lepping around the lake in the sunshine, and skipped into the water. Local men sometimes set traps for him, night-lines tied to a big log and baited with small trout and chicken and fish heads and anything else they thought might tempt the pike. They often caught big pike on those lines, but never the king of them all. I wondered if he was still down there in the deep water, his big eyes looking around for anything that might come his way, and if he was there, would he eat Uncle Patsy? I know Patsy was still in the van, but the pike might get a pull on his arm, floating out the window like he was waving the car behind to overtake him, and yank him fully out. At least that was better than the crows having a peck at you while you were whispering for a drink, and the maggots and all the rest that I didn't want to think about any more, but I couldn't help it. I saved Uncle Patsy all that at least, and he didn't deserve it because, like Da said, he was a mean hoor.

I fell asleep for a while then, and when I woke up I could hear a siren of a police car or an ambulance. The Reillys got home from Christmas Day Mass, saw the hole in the wall and the car tracks to the lake, and knew it wasn't Santy's sleigh. Even at that stage I knew I could still just walk over the fields to where all the neighbours and ambulance men were, like I was in shock, and be brought off to hospital. A warm bed and nice food. Who could ever say what happened? I could pretend I had lost my voice, or my memory, in the horrible accident that had taken away poor Uncle Patsy, who never even hurt so much as a fly.

'That poor wee child. What a terrible, terrible shock he must have had. And now to lose his Uncle Patsy too, after all that's happened already. Poor wee craythur. God knows he was a bit of a quare fish as well, but sayin' that, sure he's still only a child after all.'

Then out with the rosary beads and the novenas and the vigils and the saints' relics and the brown scapulars and the benedictions and the stations of the cross and the faces like statues and the crucifix that was blessed by His Holiness Pope Holy the Holy Third. And then the Mother of All Sorrows telling me I wouldn't be allowed to see my own mother, that I might only upset her. Upset her? How exactly? By asking her if we could just go on home and try to put this whole sorry story down to bad luck and start to get on to the next part of our life, which might turn out to be a better part? It would be better straight away, because at least me and Mammy would be together again, and back in our own house and in our own beds. Eating at our own table, and off our own plates. Saying goodnight and good morning to each other. That would sure be a whole lot better than her being bullied around by a nun who looked like a black cloud full of cold rain, who didn't care how much my mother smelled of ancient piss. And me, stuffed to the gills with hay, halfway up a chimney in a haunted ruined castle. And my dead da in so many parts that he's not so much as even buried yet, just a big jigsaw on the Sergeant's desk. I knew it was going to be left up to me to gather what was left of my family and bring them back to where they belonged. That's what I wanted for Christmas, and if Santy and God couldn't manage it between them, then I'd just have to go ahead and figure out a way to do it myself.

I'm running through a wood in the dark, but there's enough moon coming in from over my head somewhere to let me see a bit in front of me. Something screeches, first like a rat or a mouse caught in a trap with its nose smashed, but not dead, and then more like a person in bad pain. Something flies up in front of me, flapping big wings. It's a huge bird, a kind of owl, and it's got something dangling from its sharp black talons. I'm trying to see what it's caught, but it flies right up at me, staring like mad, with big angry eyes. There's blood on its curved beak and all over the feathers of its face. I think it's going to attack me, but then it swoops up at the last second and goes over my head. I turn to look after it, and then I see what it has in its claws; it's my Uncle Patsy. Only he's not dead, though he might as well be. His face is half-ripped off, and some of his insides are hanging out, but when he sees me, he reaches his hand out a bit and says, 'Help me, JJ.'

The bird circles once over me, and it hears Patsy calling to me. It reaches back with its beak as it flies and cracks Patsy's head with one crunch. Patsy's arms and legs flop and dangle limp from him, and something warm splashes my face.

Then I follow the bird's flight to see where it lands. It takes me a while to get there, and when I find the tree, there's a lot of owl pellets under it. There's a fresh one in a beam of moonlight. I recognise bits of Patsy's old jacket in the pellet, which is full of big bones. In the middle of the pellet are Patsy's rosary beads and his false teeth.

My da's watch chain is in another pellet. Then I hear the bird coming back with another human in its claws, but I can't see who it is.

FOURTEEN

I KEPT WORKING AWAY ON MY new hideout all the time. I cleared out the big fireplace, and made a bed there. It wasn't much of a bed, but I used clumps of leaves and stuff that was in the chimney, and fresh hay that I'd robbed from a cattle feeder in the next field. I still didn't want to go too far from the castle, even in the dark, in case they were looking for me. I used some of the briars and branches to block up the way that I'd come in. I figured if they brought down hunting dogs to look for me, the dogs would smell my trail out, briars or no briars. Poor Spinner would give me away without meaning to. I decided to try not to go in and out that way. It'd be safer using the chimney if I could make a way in and out through that.

The chimney was wide, and I worked my way up inside it by keeping my back to one side, and then sort of walking in little baba steps up the far wall. It was slow, and it was sore on my back. I suppose the men who built those castles never expected anyone to be inspecting the inside of the chimney, so they didn't mind if they made a hames of that part. It was full of sharp stones sticking out at all angles, and each time I inched up a bit, I had to spend a few minutes trying to set my back in a way that wouldn't cut a hole in me, and leave half my innards below in the grate.

First it came out into another big fireplace, on the next floor of the castle. This fireplace was smaller, but still big enough for me to sit or sleep in. It was half covered-in at the front, where the hearth should be, from stones and dust that had fallen down when the roof had collapsed, and it was like a little stone igloo, or one of those wee stone huts the old monks used to do their confessions in. I could go up there if I was being attacked, and throw the rocks down at anyone who tried to follow me up the chimney. Farther on up the chimney, there was a big branch or a root or something. I grabbed it to pull myself up, and as soon as I did, something started to move above me. Dust and stones started to come down. A few big stones whacked off me and nearly knocked me all the way back down. There were more stones and dust, with a noise like hailstones. Then one big crash that shook the whole castle. I thought it all was coming down, and me only after moving in. Either that, or I had woken up the ghost who haunted the place.

Then it all just stopped. I was covered in dirt and dust, and my head was sore from a few big stones that had hit me on their way down, but the chimney was still there, and I'd managed to keep holding on in the chimney wall. It was dark over my head, and I knew something big had moved up there. I climbed the rest of the way. The gap in the chimney was blocked with one big rock that had fallen from somewhere up higher, but couldn't fit down the hole. Lucky for me, or I'd have been as squelched as Donal Hannigan's terrier Titch when it went under Con Boylan's milk lorry.

There were a few gaps knocked out in the side, though, and I could see pretty well once I reached out and cleared away some weeds and leaves. It was a perfect lookout tower. I could see right down to the lake on one side, and then back towards town through another spyhole in the chimney wall. I could see over to the hill where my own house was from another crack in the chimney. Some of the stones were loose enough for me to push them out and wiggle through the gap in an emergency. Now that I had a big slab of rock over the top of the chimney, the rain couldn't get in.

I kept well out of the way on the first day. I could see a lot of gardaí around the place, on and off. They had their frog-gardaí in the lake again, just like when they were looking for my da. Except this time they were on the right track. I'd say the frog-gardaí were bucking mad that they'd had to leave their lovely hot Christmas dinners and go and shiver their backsides off in a freezing cold lake. Well, I didn't ask them to be frog-gardaí.

'Hey, lads, if you're looking for my uncle, Patsy Rooney, the good news is he's down there about eighty or ninety feet. The bad news is that the eels have probably moved in by now, and I'd say they have half the head gone off him already. It's Christmas in fish-land too. Oh yes, and the big pike had the other half. Poor old Patsy. I believe he died of a terrible dose of bad steering. That, and a holy water font.'

Eventually a big truck with a crane arrived, and after a few hours the frog-gardaí attached chains to Patsy's van, and they pulled it up out of the lake, spewing water through every gap and crack. I was still wondering if he would start roaring when the water had all drained away, 'I'll kill that little bastard' or something, but the van was lowered onto the lake shore quietly as far as I could hear, and nobody jumped out the driver's door when it reached the ground. Then I saw a hearse drive up. It was raining a bit, and it was starting to get dark by then, but the gardaí had lights on from the squad cars to help them see. Then a fire engine came, and an ambulance. Knowing the cut of Uncle Patsy before he'd finally glugged under, I couldn't see the point in having an ambulance at that stage, not even if God Himself was driving it, but then I thought it must be there in case anyone would vomit when they saw Patsy with his big swollen-up head, and half his guts wrapped around the magnetic statue of Saint Martin de Porres on the dashboard.

Then, last of all, Father Nealon drove up. He must have waited to finish his Christmas dinner. He went around to the driver's side of the van and I suppose he said a prayer or two.

'Bless poor Patsy, Oh Lord we pray, now let me home to finish me tay.'

They were all back and forth for a good while. My hideout in the castle chimney was about a length and a half of a football field away, so I couldn't really see what was going on, but eventually they took a coffin out of the hearse, and after a few minutes they put it back in again. Then they took a stretcher out of the ambulance, and went round the far side of the van with it. After a while they came back out with the stretcher, with a big mound on it, covered in a blanket or something, and four men carrying it. One of the men had to be replaced before they got to the ambulance, because I could see him bent over double and holding the side of the van. I often saw Da that way after coming home late from hiding. It was probably from Da being curled up in a ball someplace all day, trying not to be found, and not eating or anything, that he was often so sick. My mam often said then that it was no wonder he was sick, and that he couldn't go on much longer the way he was.

They had to get another man for the stretcher then, when a second lad went double a minute later. It reminded me of a poem Brother Callary at the school used to recite sometimes. It was called 'Horatio on the Bridge', and it was about soldiers trying to chop down a wooden bridge

113

before the enemy got across to murder them all. The enemy were on one side, blasting away for all they were worth, and Horatio's men were on the other side, chopping like billy-o. Every time one of Horatio's men got an arrow in the belly, another lad stepped up to take his place. About halfway through the poem, there was as many lads floating in the river as there was left above on the bank. The river was turned red from all the poor dead choppers. Anyway, the bridge fell in the end, and the lads who were left said what a great day it was. The enemy stood there with their hands on their hips for a while, not sure what to do next. They probably shouted a few last curses across the river, 'Yez bastards. We'll get yez yet, but,' and then went home for their tea.

'Patsy always had that effect on me too, lads,' I wanted to shout down to the men who were getting sick from my castle on the hill.

Then the ambulance and the hearse drove away, and the fire engine, and one of the garda cars went with them. The poor frog-gardaí who were left behind were freezing I'd say, and probably wanted to go and drink a few pints of beer someplace warm, except the pubs wouldn't be open on Christmas Day. But I knew what was really keeping them all there – me. Where was that boy?

'The man's wee nephew was with him in the car, going home to have Christmas dinner with his uncle. So where is he? Because he wasn't in the car when we brought it up, and the door on the passenger side was bent shut so no man, let alone an eleven- year-old boy, could open it. He could have climbed out the broken window maybe, but he was surely unconscious by the time the car hit the water, considering what it did to that wall on the way in. Maybe he just floated off out the broken window, and kept sinking to the deepest part of that lake. It could be a long time before he bobs back up. Anyway, it's near dark, and the dinner's only half-ate. We may all go home.'

They got back into the water again after a while. They were up and down like otters for the last bit of light that was left, and I thought they'd never go, but it started to get too dark even for the frog-gardaí and when they couldn't see anything, they finally packed up and left. Then I was able to go and find some Christmas supper.

FIFTEEN

REILLY'S HENS LAID ALL OVER THE place, in every ditch and hollow for half a mile. I don't even know why old Phil Reilly bothered to keep hens at all, because he surely never got more than three or four eggs a year from them. I think he couldn't catch the hens to eat them, and they just kept on scratching and craw-cawing and laying eggs and wandering all around as if they owned the place. Now and then one of them would get eaten by a fox, or plastered to the road by a truck, but there was still a lot of hens around no matter what. I always knew where to find those eggs, because sometimes when I'd be out fishing the lake with my da, or just tricking about with Spinner in the fields around Reilly's farm, I'd come on a spot where old Reilly's hens would be after laying a few eggs. I even brought a few home to Mammy once, but she told me to leave them back where I'd got them, that God didn't like stealing.

'But, Mam, God doesn't like waste either, you always say,' which is exactly what she'd tell me if I didn't eat everything on my plate.

'Oh, the devil can cite scripture, surely.'

That was all she'd answer if I said anything with God in it that she didn't like. I hadn't the faintest idea what it was supposed to mean, so I sometimes used the eggs for target practice. I'd sneak out my da's old pellet gun and shoot the eggs off a wall, or else I'd just throw eggs at the cows.

So I knew how to find a few eggs around the place, even at night, when it was safe for me to come out. The only thing was you'd never know exactly when they were laid, so you could get a fairly rotten one here and there, a smell that would turn your stomach something treacherous.

When Gickna from the home was really, really hungry, he used to say, 'I'd eat a scabby donkey.' I don't think he had ever even seen an ordinary donkey, never mind a scabby one, but I knew what he meant. The first few days after Patsy's accident I was too hungry to care what I ate. If there was a hoor's ghost in the castle, I'd have eaten that too. That was one of Da's favourite curses for people he didn't like – he'd call them a hoor's ghost. Mam didn't like it at all, so I never said it, but things had changed between me and my mam, and I was learning a lot about the world, and I wasn't going to do what everyone wanted any more. Look where it had got me so far – pushed around, locked up, sat on, and told nothing.

'From now on, things are going to be done JJ's way,' I said half out loud. I couldn't make a worse hames of it than the adults had, I knew that much.

So I got a few eggs from Reilly's stray hens that Christmas night. I also found a frozen chunk of milk in the bottom of a milk churn at the end of the lane. The churn hadn't been washed out, I suppose because it was Christmas, and then with Uncle Patsy smashing down their wall and drowning himself, Phil Reilly probably just forgot entirely about wee jobs like rinsing out the milk churn. I was going to bring the frozen milk back to the castle in the lid of the churn, but I didn't want to start any suspicions with things going missing around the place. So I hunted about till I found an old plastic container in the ditch. I didn't much like the smell out of it, so I washed it in the little stream that ran by the ditch and into the lake, and then I crushed the chunk of frozen milk down into the opening. It was easy enough because it started to melt a bit with the heat of my hands. Then I headed back, before some hoor's ghost heard me and started poking around. I got into my bed, cracked the eggs into the plastic carton, swished them all around till the milk was more or less all melted and the eggs were sort of scrambled, and I drank the whole lot. It wasn't the best Christmas dinner I'd ever had, but I preferred it to Pasty's soggy spuds, or fat Hilary's turkey, with five lectures for dessert. And then her arse on top of me, trying to squeeze it all back out of me again because I asked her if she'd eaten all her family. No, at last now I was king of the castle. My castle.

'Castle JJ – keep out, or prepare to meet your own guts.'

I was starting to feel pretty tired, but I had one more thing to do before I could risk going to sleep. I needed to have something to defend myself with, in case anyone found my hideout before I had time to make more escape tunnels in and out. If I woke up suddenly and there was a neighbour standing over me, ready to start shouting, 'I have the wee murdering hoor, I have him trapped,' and giving the whole game away, then I'd need a good weapon to silence his gob quick. There were plenty of sticks around, and a few of them had good sharp pointy ends where they broke. I could only feel for them, because it was pitch dark by then, except for a scutty bit of a moon, but I got a few sticks that felt like good ones for pushing into an eye, or down a big gawking mouth, and filling it with bark before words could get out and snare me like Brer Rabbit. When it was light again, I'd get the best sharp sticks, and make a few piles of them, near every way in and every way out. Then if more than one neighbour came sniffing, I could keep them all quiet. Nobody can give you away when they have a branch through their Adam's apple, and it would serve them right for interfering in my family. They'd all be better off praying that the frost wouldn't wipe out the geraniums or something, and not getting involved in things that were my business. Then, when I'd have a brace or two of the hoors killed and threaded along a sharp stick, like Da used to do with the perch we'd catch, I could maybe hide their bodies in the lake, and hope that everyone would think the whole place was really cursed and haunted for sure, and keep away. Or else, if they figured out it was me all along, I'd just do what Egg said: 'Run like fuck.'

So that's what I got for my second Christmas without my da: a dead uncle, a hay suit, a castle, sour eggs and frozen milk mixed with a bit of stuff for liver fluke, and five sticks with sharp ends to blind intruders. And then, like all good boys who've had a very busy Christmas Day, I fell fast asleep.

I'm at home helping Mam to give the Christmas cake mix a few extra stirs of the wooden spoon in the big bowl she only uses for Christmas baking. Da is laughing because I can't stir the thick mixture. He stands beside me and squeezes my muscles, which makes me laugh, even though it sort of hurts a bit too, and then he takes my hand that's holding the wooden spoon, and we stir the cake mix together, and it goes round and round like there's only water in the bowl.

'I've seen more meat on a butcher's pencil on a Good Friday,' Da says, laughing and grabbing my arm again.

'Aren't you a lucky woman now that has two big strong fellas like us to protect you?' he says to my mam, and then chases her around the table a few times with the wooden spoon, all gooey and sticky with cake stuff. Mam screams and laughs at the same time, and Da goes 'Fee Fi Fo Fum' as he chases her.

SIXTEEN

I TRIED TO COUNT THE DAYS, so I would know how much time was going by, but it was hard to be sure after the first few. I slept for short spells during the day, because I always woke up feeling cold and shivery. I couldn't go out during the day anyway, and when I'd open my eyes, I'd start to get mixed up about whether it was the same day, or if I'd slept right through to the next. I got to know by the people moving around in Reilly's farm, and on the roads, more or less if it was morning or afternoon. The days were short, which was good, because I was usually weak with hunger by the time night came. There were still people coming and going around the lake for a few days, and I had to keep very quiet while all that was still going on.

Crows thought they owned my castle. They were always on the chimney and the walls. I didn't mind the noise of them too much – in fact they were a good alarm if anything was coming near the castle, because they'd fly up and make a terrible ruction. But I couldn't stop thinking that some of those crows might be the same lads that ate my da's eyes, or hopped around inside his ribcage, tearing strips off in there. I thought it would only be fair if I could get my own back by eating a few of them. They were handy enough to catch at night when they were roosting, and I got good at grabbing crows in the dark. I could only get one at a time, because they'd squawk so much when I'd grab one, they'd frighten all the others off into the night. I had no way to cook them, though, and I wasn't going to risk a fire, even though I lived in a chimney.

The raw taste was strange for the first couple of times, and I even vomited up a few crow bits, like an owl's pellet. But I was hungry all the time, and the bastards were after eating my da, so I stuck at it till I got used to it. Then it was grand. That's how hawks and owls and foxes live, and it doesn't do them any harm.

One night I found one of old Reilly's chickens roosting in a bit of a bush, and I got it and broke its neck without a sound. I had to hold it tight for a few minutes then, because it was more lively with its neck broken and nearly clean off, than most chickens are when their necks are grand. It was much easier than climbing all over the castle in the dark trying to catch scrawny crows, and there's a lot more meat on a chicken. I used sharp sticks to break up the meat, but I still wished I had a knife to cut things with. I could put a better point on the sticks too, though by then I had a good collection of sharp sticks of all shapes and sizes.

I felt like Robinson Crusoe, only I didn't have any coconuts to make little bombs with. All the time I kept clearing new spaces to lie in or to watch from. I could go right around the castle in the dark after a few weeks without ever bumping into anything. I could pop up anywhere, and then disappear in a second. All the old stories about the castle being haunted were true; I was the ghost.

One day I was pulling a big tree root out of the way, when the ground caved in under me, and I fell into a hole in the castle floor. The hole was just big enough for me to stand up in, and at first I thought it was a trap, that the neighbours knew I was there all the time, and that they had waited to catch me in a snare. But when all the falling stones and mud and dust settled, nobody came over to the hole saying, 'Now we have ye, ye little murdering shitehawk.'

I got up and cleared a few branches and roots out of the way, and there was just a dark tunnel going off somewhere, but I couldn't see where. I stepped down into the tunnel and walked a few steps into the dark with my hands stretched out in front of me, feeling my way. It seemed like it went on for ever, so I decided to come back out before I got lost or trapped down there, and plan what I'd do next.

I was shaking and so excited that I said out loud, 'This could be the hideout to beat all hideouts.' I gave myself a fright, hearing my own voice. I hadn't said one word out loud since whatever was the last thing I'd said to my mortally wounded Uncle Patsy as I crawled out of the lake on Christmas Day. But I knew this was an important discovery, like the man we learned about in school, who realised that if you climb into a bath full of water, the amount of water that winds up on the floor is the same size as you are. He got so excited, he jumped straight out of the bath, and he was so keen to tell everyone, he forgot he was in the nude. I felt like him. Maybe it was a secret escape tunnel for the king who lived in the castle long ago, in which case probably nobody on earth knew it was there, or where the tunnel might come out. And now it was mine, part of a place where nobody could get at me and make me go anywhere or do anything that I didn't want to. They all thought I was as dead as a dodo bird, as my da used to say, but here I was, with my own castle with secret underground burrows, and me dining on raw chicken and crow's blood, just like the real ghost of a great dead murdered king, hungry for revenge.

King JJ the First, Lord of Tunnels, Houdini of Piggery Hill and Ghost of Burrow Castle.

I knew that I needed a few things to explore the burrows with properly – tools. That meant risking a trip to my old house. It was only across a few fields, and I knew from watching at night that there wasn't anybody going in or staying there, because I never saw a light or a lamp on in the place. I could break in where nobody would see any marks, take whatever I needed – knives and forks, a tin opener and a few tins of whatever was left in the press, and a flash lamp that my da had for checking the yard at night. There was a blowtorch as well, and if I could find that, I could maybe use it to cook the crow meat a bit. Or burn the eyes out of the nosey hoors.

I didn't know for sure if there were batteries in the flashlamp, or if they'd even work if there was, but I could look around, and Da usually kept some extra ones in the big dresser. I badly needed warm clothes too. I decided I'd only take old clothes of my da's, in case anyone happened to see that mine were gone, and get suspicious. Old Mother of All Sorrows might come snooping to see if anyone had left a few pounds lying about, and smell that something was up. I could puff Da's clothes out with a bit of straw, and if anyone ever did happen to catch a sight of me one night, well they'd think I was just some old drunk piddling in the ditch. And I'd take anything else that looked like it might come in handy. The shotgun was surely gone after the siege in the summer, but the pellet gun was maybe still there, tucked safely away in the attic. It would be grand for rabbits the odd time, because it wasn't too loud. I could use it in an emergency on a curious neighbour too. A pellet in one eye and a blast of the blowtorch in the other would stop anyone long enough for me to run and hide again.

Rabbits, nosey neighbours and hoor's ghosts.

SEVENTEEN

'BLESS THIS HOUSE'. THAT WAS A little wooden sign in the kitchen of our home. I bought it in town one time with my da, with some money I'd saved. I gave it to Mammy for Mother's Day. She was thrilled with it, and she took down a picture of a mountain that was on the wall, and put up my 'Bless This House' sign instead. Everyone who came to visit us for months after that was shown the sign, and they all said I was a very kind boy to buy such a nice present for my mammy. Some of the visitors even said that I'd probably end up being a priest.

I saw the way Mammy looked at me when the visitors said it, so I smiled and said I was going to become one as soon as I was old enough. Then some of the old women would slip a coin into my hand, and pat my head, and say, 'God bless you, child.' I figured it wasn't doing any harm really, since it made them all so happy, and most of them were so old, they'd probably be long dead before they'd realise that I had no intention of becoming a priest.

The clock in the kitchen was silent. It usually made a loud ticking noise that used to drive my da mad when he was trying to have a nap or read the newspaper. Mam said that it helped to remind us that our time here on earth was precious, but sometimes Da would stop the pendulum, and say that his time would be even more precious if he could have a look at the paper in peace.

It was easy to get in our back door, because it would never shut right in the winter once the rain got into it, and you couldn't lock it. Besides, who'd be interested in robbing our old house anyway? All Uncle Patsy ever wanted was the farm, and I don't think he cared what happened to the house. He'd probably have put pigs in it if his plan had worked out. I left my shoes outside the back door, so as not to leave any mucky marks as evidence inside. I knew the house so well, I could have gone through it with my eyes closed, so the dark didn't really bother me, and I started to see things a bit better after a few minutes in there anyway.

I tried for Da's old flash lamp first. He kept it on a high shelf above the back door, and I needed a chair from the kitchen to reach up. It was still there. I tried the switch on it, but the batteries were dead, and there were no spare batteries on the shelf. I took it down and opened it to get out the old batteries, and I found a small bottle with something strong like whiskey inside the middle of the torch, where the batteries should have been. Adults sometimes had whiskey when they were cold, so I decided to bring it with me, and maybe try a bit. My old fishing bag was with some coats and wellingtons and fishing rods inside the back door, and I put the torch and the bottle into that. I had a little penknife in my fishing bag for cutting line, but I wanted a bigger knife too, so I went to the drawer in the kitchen.

Everything was just like it was when we all lived there before, except the range wasn't lit. When Mammy was in the house, the range never went out, and the kettle was never off the boil. People were always calling by and having tea and big long chats with my mother. I found her big knife that Da used to carve the roast with on a Sunday, and a few smaller knives that she had for peeling potatoes and things. Da used to say they were for keeping your eyes peeled. There was the tin opener, and the big wooden spoon that Da belted me with a few times when he was in a very bad mood. I just took the big knife, one small one, and the tin opener, and put them in the fishing-tackle bag. There was a sharpening stone in the drawer, and I took that to keep all my knives ready for cutting.

It was strange being in my parents' bedroom, because I don't think I'd ever been in there on my own before, except maybe when I was five and had the measles. Back then Mam had hung an old blanket thing on the big light shade over the bed in their room, because I couldn't take the light.

The bed was still made, all tidy the way Mam liked everything to be, and there was even one of her cardigans over the back of the chair, as if she had just gone out to lock up the hens for the night, and would be back any minute. I opened their wardrobe and pulled out a few of Da's jumpers and jackets, and some vests and socks. I put on two jackets and two jumpers, and left his big overcoat back by the door, to bring when I was ready to go. Everything had a stale smell, like pissy sheets that Mam hadn't found, and they were all damp. The overcoat felt very heavy, and I found another bottle in the pocket. That one was empty, so I put it back into the wardrobe.

Then I got a chair and climbed up into the attic. I couldn't see a thing because it was pitch black up there – not even a screed of moonlight getting in – but the attic was small, and I found what I wanted by feeling around for a bit. The pellet gun was there, just inside the attic door. I'd seen Da put it up there after using it on crows or pigeons, or after he'd let me use it to shoot tin cans or eggs off the wall, so

I knew where to look. There was a box of pellets beside it. I'd seen a couple of rats around the castle, and I didn't want them spoiling the food, so I could get them with the pellet gun too. There were candles there too that I'd forgotten about till I felt them in my hand beside the gun. Da always kept a few candles for when there was a power cut. I took the pellet gun and a box of lead pellets and the candles, and closed up the attic.

I looked into my old bedroom. It was strange to be back there after so long. Or maybe it wasn't really that long, but so much was after happening, it felt like ages. I still had no matches for the candles, but the moon was lighting up my bedroom and I could see things fairly well. It looked like nobody had been there since the Famine. Mammy had always been too busy praying to go into my bedroom and check if it was tidy. I felt woeful sad for a minute, but I stopped myself because I had too many things to do, and I had to get back to my castle as fast as I could.

There wasn't much that I wanted to take from my own room. I had an Action Man that I liked, and a comic annual, but I didn't know where they were and I didn't have time to start rooting around for them. I found a pair of binoculars that Da used for spotting rabbits or pigeons when he'd go hunting. I didn't really mind him shooting those pigeons, because he said they were vermin, but I didn't like him shooting the rabbits. I made noise a few times when I was out with him, to help them to escape, and once when I did it Da belted me and sent me home. Well, the rabbits might have to die now, I thought, to keep JJ alive. Da would let me have the binoculars in my own room when he didn't need them.

I wanted to look around more, and I even thought about sleeping in the house, just for one night. After all, it was my house. But I decided not to, not yet anyway. I got a few more things in the presses downstairs: a scissors, string, packets of soup and packets of jelly, a tin mug. I couldn't carry too much, and I didn't want to be seen going across the fields with half the house on my back. In a drawer full of all sorts of junk I found a few loose batteries. I took them, and hoped they would fit the torch, and still work. I stuffed all that would fit into my fishing bag, and the rest into the pockets of Da's overcoat and jackets. Then I took down the 'Bless This House' sign, and put that in my bag too. I couldn't find the blowtorch, so there was no Sunday roast jackdaw to look forward to.

I got a fright just when I was going out. I thought I heard my mam asking me what I'd like for tea, just as I was closing the back door behind me.

'Ants' kneecaps and spiders' toenails,' I said, but only in a whisper.

EIGHTEEN

THE TUNNELS WERE LIKE A RABBIT'S warren that maybe went on for miles. I still hadn't gone all the way to the end of even one of them, and there were three. The flash lamp was a bit weak, because none of the batteries from the house were new. They were kind of rusted a bit, and the lamp kept flickering. I wanted to save them as much as I could, so I went slowly in the dark for a few yards, then turned the torch on again to get another look ahead, then turned it off again to save the batteries. It was cold and damp in the tunnels, but now at least I was warm with Da's clothes and socks, and a pair of wellies I'd taken from the back door. One of the wellies had more whiskey in the bottom of it, in a small bottle, like I sometimes saw Da putting in his tea.

I was sorry I didn't try to find some matches in the house, because I could have used the candles and saved the flash lamp. Or I'd have been able to risk making a small fire down in the tunnel, because it was surely long enough to hide any smoke. I put matches down on my shopping list for the next visit home.

One day, or night, I wasn't sure any more, I found a place where two of the tunnels connected, and there was a big open place, like a room, wide enough to live in if the weather got too bad above ground. Or if I got Mammy to come and stay with me.

I knew by then that we would never last long in our own house, not against all the interfering liars who were out to stop us getting our family together again. That is, if I could even get Mam back there in the first place, but Da always said where there's a will there's a way. And another siege would be a waste of time. All I had now was a pellet gun and a few knives and sticks, and Mammy was so astray in her head that I couldn't rely on her not to be a traitor again, and invite them all in like before. Except Uncle Patsy wouldn't be kicking down any more doors; he was too busy shovelling coal for the devil. I figured I'd need a good long while alone with her to explain everything, and not have interruptions from smiling thieves and very holy liars who didn't want the truth ever to come out. The tunnels would be the perfect place, perfect for me and Mam to begin to get back to our old life, and for me to be able to explain everything to her clearly. Then when my mother understood everything, and the spell or the bad medicine they gave her had worn off, we could go back to our old house together, and Mammy could tell them all to go and fly a kite, that she was looking after her boy JJ again. It wouldn't be the most comfortable place Mammy was ever in, down the tunnels, but she always said that she didn't care for comforts, as long as she had her family around her.

So I started to settle that part of the tunnels a bit for my mam, to make it nice. I made a couple more trips to our old house over the next few weeks, not too regular to risk being spotted, but I never took much stuff back at one time. I'd go up to the chimney lookout first and have a good check around before going anywhere. I got to know the local sounds of people coming and going, and I more or less knew when the neighbours were settled down for the night, and when it was safe to go out. I got some more little things at our house that I knew Mam liked, favourite clothes of hers, and a blanket to sleep in. I couldn't expect her to sleep in a bed of twigs and hay, and the chair she liked to sit in by the range was too big for me to carry. Besides, if anyone came in to check on the house, they might miss it and start asking the Sergeant around. Every time I brought back some new things, I settled the place up a bit more, the way I thought she'd like it.

I even hung the 'Bless This House' sign from a big rusty steel ring that was sticking in through the wall of the big round room, just to remind her of home. I knew she wouldn't want to eat crows, at least not crows that weren't even cooked, so I kept any tins of beans and stuff that I took from the house in a little pantry in the tunnel, especially for her. After the slops she was probably getting in the convent place, baked beans would taste delicious. I found a few more batteries for the flash lamp too, and two new ones still in plastic in a toolbox on top of Da's wardrobe. There was some paper money there, and I took it too. It wasn't stealing – it belonged to my family. I was only minding it for my mammy, till we'd be back at home eventually, and we'd need to do a proper shopping in town, and give up crows and baked beans.

All the time I was doing up the tunnel like home, I was thinking of ways to get Mam out of that convent place. I wasn't certain that she was even still there. Only once did I catch a glimpse of her. It was fairly early one rainy morning, and I was doing my daily checking around with the binoculars. There was a line of people walking behind the priest along the road to the graveyard. There wasn't that many people living around our place, so I was wondering who was dead. I moved to the other side of the chimney, and I could watch them till they got up to fairly near the graveyard. Then just before I lost sight of them behind some trees, I saw Mammy getting out of a black car, and she was all in black too, and Father Nealon came over and took her by the two hands. Then a coffin came out of another car, but Mam didn't go to watch it being buried. She got back in the black car, and she stayed there till it was all over. Then Father Nealon came back and drove them all off again. I wanted to run across the fields, wave the car down and jump in beside Mammy and hug her and tell her I was grand, and that my skull wasn't a hotel for eels at the bottom of the lake, like everyone thought. But I knew I couldn't, not yet anyway. I knew she wasn't ready. I badly wanted to see her, but it was broad daylight, and even if I could sneak over without being spotted, I could be sure Mam would kick up a racket when she'd see me. I was too afraid. After everything that had happened, my mother might start crying and get me caught. That would be the end of all my plans, and we would never be together again.

Up till then, from when Uncle Patsy had broken the land speed record coming down Piggery Hill at Christmas, I hadn't been too far from Castle JJ, so I wasn't too sure any more exactly what was going on in the town. Mostly I was just in the fields around Phil Reilly's farm at night, because the castle was on his land. So were the eggs and milk that I mostly lived on. And Phil was a bit blind I think, so even if he was out in his yard relieving himself at night after he'd had a few bottles of stout, and happened to catch sight of me, he wouldn't know who I was.

Sometimes old Spinner started to bark. Phil Reilly kept Spinner tied up at night in the spring so he wouldn't worry sheep at lambing time. I think Spinner could smell me in the wind, and he badly wanted me to scratch his tummy and trick about like we used to do. Go down to the Weal maybe, and chase me along the bank while I'd bomb down the fast water on a fat tube, but I couldn't explain it all to a big thick of a dog. I couldn't even explain to my own mam. Maybe Spinner wanted me to understand something too. Maybe he wanted to say that it was not him that ate my da. Well, I already knew that. Spinner and me were old pals, and he wouldn't do that to his pal's da.

The farthest I'd gone was to my own house. If I was going to get my mam back first, then I'd have to risk a trip across ten or twelve fields to the convent, or to the Fairy Fort that was made to look like a convent, where she was being kept. For once the road to the place would actually have been shorter, but it was far too dangerous.

Getting there was one thing, but then how was I going to get her to come back with me, without her making a big racket and getting us caught? I wished my tunnels came up under the convent. Then I could pop up from under the floor in the middle of the night, grab Mammy while she was still too sleepy to know what was going on, and disappear again into thin air before Mother of the Sorrowful Mysteries got wind that anything was wrong.

I put the new batteries in the torch and went as far as I could get in the tunnels. One was collapsed in completely a few yards down into it, probably from milk trucks, tractors, combine harvesters and bailers, or big scutter-arsed heifers giving each other piggybacks in the field above. Or maybe the same lads who had built the chimney in the castle that nearly cut the back off me had built the tunnels too, and they were a bit lazy and didn't use enough cement. Anyway that tunnel was no good. I saw a few more rats. They thought they owned the place too, the way they'd just sit staring at me. Another tunnel went down very steep after a while. It was a bit like I was on the inside of Piggery Hill, and maybe I was, because then the ground got really wet, and I finally figured out that I must be near the lake.

The old king, whoever he was, had an escape tunnel down to the water, and I guessed he had a boat there to whisk him away somewhere safe if his enemies took over his castle. Me and that king would have had a lot to talk about, if we could ever have met, because we thought about things the same way, so we did. I figured that if his ghost was still wandering around the castle, I'd have been only too happy to sit down and pluck a few crows with him.

This was the tunnel that connected to the big room, and then I thought maybe the room was where the king hid his escape boat, and he tied it to the steel ring in the wall. Sure, if his enemies saw his boat sitting outside a tunnel in the lake, they'd only put a hole in the boat, and send a few lads up the tunnel to meet the king coming down it, before wrecking his castle.

NINETEEN

I NEVER THOUGHT I'D BE THANKING the fairies for anything, but they solved a big problem for me, even if they weren't really trying to help me. There hadn't been any frost for a few weeks, so I knew it was coming well into spring. It was brighter in the evenings too, so I had to wait before I could get out to hunt. That didn't bother me though, because I had plenty of food stored up in the castle by then, and I didn't have to wait till the night-time to eat.

This one evening I was checking from my lookout chimney before going out, when I saw a kind of white figure moving in a field over by our house. I got the binoculars, but the light was bad, and the figure was moving in and out between trees and ditches, so I couldn't get a proper look at it.

I thought it might be a will-o'-the-wisp, like my mother often told me about, that moves about the bogs and fields. She said they were hopeless souls who couldn't get into Heaven because they did some very bad thing in their lifetime, or they wouldn't let the priest in to see them on their deathbed, and so they just roamed the earth for all eternity. Sometimes they would lead an innocent person to their death across the bog and into a bog hole, because they were just fed up and had nothing better to do, and the more people who were as miserable as themselves, the better. So I was not going to be taken in by a will-o'-the-wisp, but I kept watching it anyhow. It went right up to our old house, and stood there for a long while. Then I thought it might be Uncle Patsy, coming around to see if he could coax me to go for a nice long walk over the blasted bogs with him and drown me. Or maybe it was just an ordinary robber, looking to steal whatever he could get from the house. Or else just a poor craythur looking to sleep in the barn or something. Only none of the tramps I ever saw before wore a long yellow nightdress.

The binoculars were not very good when it wasn't fully bright outside, so I knew there was only one way to solve the mystery. I headed off across the fields and through the line of ditches that ran right up around our house. I had more tunnels there, right down through the middle of the thick briars and brambles and whitethorn bushes that grew in the ditches around our farm. I had made enough room for myself over the winter nights to crawl right through, by bending back branches, with a jacket wrapped around them, and then breaking them quietly, till there was a narrow little tunnel running right up through the middle of all the ditches. I could crawl along at the bottom of the ditches, keeping real low. It was still a bit boggy after all the winter rain, but if you crawled with your hands and knees on each side, you could keep up out of the muck.

I had a few snares set for rabbits along the way. I'd watched my da often enough to know how to set them. I never really liked snares, or killing rabbits, but I had to do it to get food. All I needed for the snares was a loop of wire or strong fishing line, tied to a piece of wood stuck into the ground. If a rabbit passed through it, the loop tightened itself around his neck, just by him walking on ahead. After a bit he'd feel something strange pulling at him. When he'd try to get away, it would just keep getting tighter, and he'd choke himself to death. I was glad I didn't have to be around to see it happening, or hear the rabbits squealing. I'd probably have just let them go if I saw it, because rabbits were always being eaten by everything and I felt sorry for them. Still, they were grand to eat, and it didn't bother me so much once they were stiff dead when I found them. I just pretended to myself that they'd died of old age or a heart attack. It was a good way for getting some different food, whenever I was sick of crows. When I hunted that way with my da, he always used to skin the rabbits we caught, and so I could do that too. I kept the skins and dried them out on a long stick back at the tunnels. They were like Indian scalps. I used to look at them sometimes and pretend they belonged to all the people who had crossed me – Uncle Patsy, Mother of the Sorrowful Mysteries, fat Hilary and some of her trainee little pigs in the home, the holy neighbours, and Father Nealon too, because he pretended I could trust him but he'd tried to trick me.

Now that the leaves were growing back in all the ditches, I could stay in there even in the daytime if I wanted to, and still not be seen. So that was how I went to investigate the ghost at our old house.

It was the biggest shock of my life. There was my mammy, in her long yellow nightdress, just like during the nights the summer before. She was mumbling to herself, sort of half-praying, and half having a conversation with someone invisible, a bit like my da used to do in the jacks at night. Once I got up fairly close, I knew it was my da she was talking to, because she said, 'The tea's getting cold' and 'Come on in now, Tommy, and put your feet up to the range and rest yourself,' and all that stuff she used to go on with before. I still couldn't believe she was standing there in front of me, though, or how in hell she had managed to escape at all. I thought I was dreaming. Someone must have left a door or a window open in the convent, and Mam had felt the cool breeze on her face, and just decided to head off home. I was so happy to see her, I nearly shouted out.

Then I remembered that even though she was free, she was probably still under a spell. What would happen if she suddenly started screaming and shouting like before, and Mother Misery and fat Hilary and Father Nealon and all their friends came out from behind a bush or out of the Fairy Fort and grabbed me? Everything would be wasted; all my plans, all my patience would be wasted. So I sat down quietly and I thought as fast as my brain could think about what to do.

First of all, Mammy was not supposed to be there with me, and there would be people out looking for her very soon, if they weren't already on her trail. So I knew I didn't have much time. Second, I knew we would have to go back to the tunnels for a while, and not just go on into our own house; Mam wasn't ready for that yet. I needed time to explain everything to her about all that had happened, and to break the fairy spell and the holy hold Mother Misery had over her. I had to have more time, and someplace quiet to explain it all to her.

But how was I to get my mother to go to the tunnels? I knew she would only go if I could trick her, because I couldn't fight her all the way back to Castle JJ without being caught. So I just did what I used to do before, and I was already wearing Da's clothes.

'I'll be in now in a minute, but you'll have to come over to the lake and give me a hand with something first,' I said in the best deep voice that I could do. My twelfth birthday was coming, but my voice wasn't breaking, and I still sounded like a girl.

She looked at me, and for a few seconds I wasn't sure what was going to happen. I knew I'd have to knock her out if she screamed, and I had a sort of big plastic dwarf thing from her little garden in my hand. Even though it was me who gave her that dwarf as a present for her birthday one year, still, if she'd made me do it, I'd have done it. But then she smiled. She smiled and said, 'Is Patsy stuck again?'

Then she started to laugh, a very quiet little laugh, and she put her hand on my shoulder. I left the plastic dwarf slowly back on the ground.

'Go on so,' she said, 'till we get him out, before he catches pneumonia. The big eejit!' she said, and started laughing again quietly to herself.

I was still afraid we would be spotted, because it was pitch night, and Mam was wearing a bright nightdress, so I took off the overcoat I had on over everything else, and put it over her shoulders. I still had on two of my da's jumpers, and a jacket with the sleeves rolled up, and one of his old caps to hide my face a bit. Mammy smiled at me again, and felt for my hand in the dark, and held it and let me lead her all the way back to Castle JJ. It was getting to be like old times already.

TWENTY

THEY MUST HAVE BROUGHT ALL THE people from four or five towns to look for Mammy. It was just as well I had a good supply of rabbits and tinned food and crows in the larder, because the fields were alive with people for days. It was hardly safe even to go to the lookout chimney tower, and I decided to stay in the tunnel for a good while, till the coast was clear. This surely was a time for me to use all my skill as a hide-and-seek champion.

When I was small, I often watched cowboy films with my da on Sunday afternoons. A rich lady would be kidnapped by the Indians after they had robbed the stagecoach, and she would be taken back to the Indian chief to see what he wanted to do next. But then a posse of people from town would saddle up and ride out after them, led by the sheriff, or sometimes by the man who was going steady with the kidnapped girl. Before long, somebody would find a piece of cloth from the rich lady's dress caught on a thorn bush or a cactus plant, and the posse would know where the crafty Indians had taken her. Whenever they got tired of riding in the sweltering heat, they'd just think of another scalp being slid down the scalp pole, and they'd get a fresh burst of energy.

So that's why I brought Mam in by the lake way. No thorn bushes for a start, and if anyone followed the footsteps, or the garda sniffer dogs followed the scent, well, they'd all think Mammy had gone into the lake after her brother Patsy. Then the frog-gardaí would be back, but they wouldn't mind as much this time, because at least it wasn't Christmas Day, and the water was not so cold now either. Then they'd decide that the pike and the eels probably had Mam long gone, like her poor wee boy JJ, and go back to the frog-garda barracks for some hot tea. If the dogs came, Spinner would be glad to bring his old friends in the garda dog kennels on another trip, and they would all wind up playing again in cow-flops when the trail ran cold, as the sheriff used to say, on the bank of the lake. Then the Sergeant would slam his door and go home for his tea like before. And nobody would find a piece of cloth from Mam's nightdress stuck to a tree either.

I didn't trust her to stay put, though, once we were safely in the tunnels and out of sight. She started to act all strange on me again as soon as we got into the tunnels, and then she was off again with her blasted crying too, and her little bird noises. I was really afraid she would give the whole game away on us, so I had to take some precautions. I stayed in the tunnels with her as much as possible. I only checked up the chimney when it got dark, because they called off the search in the evenings. Once the flashlamps went dead around the fields and the road, I knew they were all done looking for the night. There was no light in the tunnels then either, so Mam couldn't start wandering off to look for some of her old pals to pounce on me again. She wasn't really any better behaved than before, at the time of the siege.

I was really annoyed and upset about that. I had to keep a sharp eye on her to stop her from running off to tell everybody about my secret hideout, and from shouting, 'Help! Help! He has me as a prisoner in the castle! Help!'

I told her I didn't mind her praying if she wanted to, but that she was not to be doing any shouting. I told her it was just till things calmed down a bit, and till I had time to explain everything to her about what had been happening since Da had gone off up that cursed tree.

But it was no use. She was not going to listen to me. She didn't like being left in the dark, or the fact that I had to put a gag on her mouth to make sure she didn't start up screaming when somebody could hear. She even got a bit down one tunnel on the second day, crawling along in the dark like a baby, and I had to drag her back. That was hard, because she was strong, and she kicked and scratched me. She kept calling me Satan, and I kept telling her that I was just JJ.

I got her back to the chamber, because she was very confused after a while in the dark and with all the fighting, and she wasn't sure which way was out or in. I told her it was for her own safety. We were both scratched and bleeding after that. She even bit me a few times, and I had no choice but to give as good as I got. I had a big clump of her hair in my hand too by the time it was all finally calm again.

I made it as comfortable as I could for her there in the dark chamber. I brought over a stool and her favourite rug that I'd got from the house, and I put the rug over her, and lifted her feet up on the stool. I left some of her other little things there beside her too, and told her again it would not be for long, but that it really depended a lot on her and when she would get sense. That's what she used to say to me when she'd send me to my room, if I was after doing something bold.

'But how long do I have to stay in my room, Mammy?'

'Well now, JJ, that just depends on how long it takes you to see sense,' she'd say.

Another thing she used to say to me when I asked her why I had to do something I didn't want to do was, 'Because that's the why.' So I had that ready too, if she started asking, 'Why, JJ? Why?'

'Because, Mammy, that's the why.'

That's just the kind of rubbish adults are always going on with. Well, she got a taste of her own medicine then. I told her we would soon be back in our own house and this would all be in the past, like a bad nightmare. I was nearly crying myself, just thinking about us getting back home again. After the fighting and me tying her up a bit, though, she was even worse than before, and she didn't seem happy that I had done a lot of work making the tunnels all neat and tidy for her, just like home. I turned on the torch a few times, to let her see how cosy I'd made things, but that only made her worse, and she started to get frantic again, looking for a way to get out. When she saw my face, she started a terrible wailing, like a banshee.

I got very angry. I turned off the torch, and then she didn't know where she was or which way to run, but she tried to run anyway, and bashed into the wall a few times. I had to flick the torch back on to find her, but then she'd see me and scream again and get up and run like a big stupid chuck with no head straight into another wall. I decided to take off the gag and see if she'd let me help her, where she was bleeding, but she only started on again about Satan.

'Get thee away from me, Satan.'

Old poison stuff out of that cursed Bible.

I explained to her that I was not Satan, but that I was her son. I remembered a bit of the Bible she used to read to me sometimes, and I thought it would help if I said that to her, since she liked the Bible so much.

'I am your son who was lost, but is found.' Then I remembered another bit of it, 'Rejoice!'

I turned on the torch and let her see my face. She was all blood where she'd hit her head, and her mouth was bleeding as well. I think some teeth were gone, not just the false ones but some of the real ones too. For a second I thought she recognised me, and she was going to give me a smile and let me clean the blood and finally explain everything. But she went totally mad then, more than ever, screaming, blood bubbles coming out of her mouth a lot in the scream. I was scared for a few seconds, and then I got very angry again, because I knew she wanted to get us caught.

'I'm not Satan. You're Satan! Shut up or I'll stuff your rosary beads down your neck, and that will shut you up.'

I couldn't take any more of it. It was dangerous and it was not very cunning, but I just started screaming too. I thought of my da doing it sometimes, and it felt good to make someone shut up.

'Look at yourself in the mirror for Christ's sake, will you? You're the one who looks like a possessed mad lunatic fucking bitch devil with blood coming out of your mouth and eyes and screams and noise like banshees, mad fucking devil bitch.'

No way would she listen to a word I said, no matter how many curses I put in. I said all the worst ones I knew. I said some of them over and over to make it worse, but it was a waste of time, with the roars out of her. It was like a fox was running across the fields with Mam's guts in its gob, trailing them over rocks and big thistles.

I put her rug over her head to stop the noise of the screams. She still kept going though, even louder, and then

I just had to use the torch once, or maybe it was a few times, quick and hard, which could have broken it because there was that noise. She stopped, and then leaned sort of forward from where she was sitting with the rug still all covering her. But at least she stopped.

'My da was right,' I said.

I had to look quick that nobody had heard all the screaming, so I went straight to the lookout chimney to see. I moved the stones that covered the spyholes, and did a check all round. There was no sign of lights or torches coming from anywhere.

It was cold but I still stayed in the chimney. There was a big moon, like all the earth was in a tunnel, and someone was shining a torch in to see what was happening. After a while I heard a squeal, like a snared rabbit, and then after a few minutes I did see a fox going along a ditch with something brown hanging from its mouth. Brer Rabbit wasn't always so clever.

I saw bats swooping past outside, and felt their shapes whooshing close over my head. I found a dead bat in my castle one night. They look like rats with wings made of skin. I wished the rats in the tunnels would fly away to another castle, because no matter how many I killed with traps or the pellet gun, more just came out of nowhere. I got to like the night-time, even though I never did when I was a boy at home in my own bed, a thousand years ago. Everything that moved about at night-time went quietly and left no trace, even after a kill.

Mam and me are going along the bank of the Weal in the middle of summer. She has a picnic basket, and we are singing a song she used to always like: 'Row, row, row your boat, gently down the stream. Merrily, merrily, merrily, merrily, life is but a dream.'

The fields are full of buttercups, and I'm throwing some into the river, and watching them bob along on the water. Mammy and me are pretending that they are little boats, and that we are sailing off to some place where we have never been before.

'Somewhere exotic,' Mammy says.

We sit down under a big old oak tree and spread out the blanket for our picnic. Then Mam calls out to my da, 'Come on and have a bite to eat, Tommy, before this son of yours wolfs the lot.'

I look over to the old oak, and Da is having a snooze under it with his cap over his face.

TWENTY-ONE

ONLY ONCE DID I HEAR ANYBODY near the castle over the next few weeks. I heard voices, and branches breaking very early one morning before it was even fully bright. The voices were around at the place where I had found my way into the castle on Christmas morning. I hadn't been using that way in or out for months, and it was well overgrown with new briars and nettles during spring and summer, so anyone looking at it would know there was no way a person could be after using it as a way in. They didn't hang around for long. Then it was quiet again.

The weather was better by then, and I didn't need to be in the tunnels as much as in the winter. I didn't really want to go down to the chamber anyway. There was no noise from down there since I'd hit her that time when she went a bit mad. It was all different now and things were after changing again. I would have felt bad there, after what happened. I kept putting lots of food in, sort of rolling it down the slope into the chamber, even though I didn't know if she was really eating it. I didn't go into the tunnel, because if she saw me she might just scream. I thought maybe she was after realising that we have to be a family again because I was so angry and cross with her, and maybe she was thinking about everything that had happened, and seeing how I was right about Uncle Patsy and Mother Misery and all the rest of them. I thought that maybe before I was just rushing her into things when she was half under a spell, and filled with lies and confusion in her head, and that she really just needed some time to herself to work it all out. Then, when she'd finally figured it all out for herself, she would come up some morning out of the tunnel, all bright and smiling, with her hair combed and her best headscarf on, and say, 'Well, well, and would you look at how big my baby has got! Come here and give your poor foolish old mother a big kiss. That is, of course, if you're not after getting too big for that kind of carry-on!'

And I would pretend at first that I was still out with her, and that I maybe was a bit too big for all that kissing and hugging your mammy carry-on, but then I'd give her forty or fifty thousand kisses, and we would go up to tear the old boards out of the windows, and off the front door of our house, and start cleaning and polishing and praying and dusting and sweeping and tidying and praying and weeding and planting and mowing and praying and milking and cooking and baking and praying and ironing and studying and sleeping, like in the good old times a year and a half or twenty years ago. I'd stay up all night with her praying, if that's what she asked me to do. I'd learn how to say Mass in Latin if she wanted me to, and become a priest, or a bishop, or a saint even, if that was what she wished for.

'We'll say a special prayer now,' she'd say when she'd be a little old lady, at the end of giving out the rosary in the church, 'to Saint JJ, Patron Saint of Crows, that he will hear all your special intentions.'

The food started to stink, so I knew she wasn't eating it. Then it suddenly occurred to me that she might be after escaping out by the lake way, that maybe that was why there hadn't been a sound out of her for the past few weeks, and I ran down the tunnel without another thought, fully expecting to find her gone. She was still where I'd left her though, too stubborn even to move from the spot. I could see with the torch that her blanket was moving a bit. It was like one of her tiny hands was going up to her face, and another hand was moving down to her leg. So I just thought, 'Have it your way so,' and I left her for another while.

'If you won't see sense and come back to the house, then this will just have to be our house from now on,' I said on the way out.

She didn't answer.

'It makes no odds to me either way,' I said, 'for I've been living here for months now, and I'm well settled.'

Still no answer.

'Fair enough so,' I said. 'If you're going to dig your heels in here, then I'm going to go and get my da and bring him to stay here with us as well. You'll just have to protect yourself from anything that comes in when I'm gone, because I can't mind you all the time. There's sometimes a bat or two in the tunnel, and I've seen the odd rat too. And before you even ask, it's because that's the why.'

She still wouldn't answer, so I went to get Da.

I'm fishing with my da in a boat on the long lake. He's laughing and joking about a fish I've caught.

'I've caught fish with bigger teeth than that,' he says, and throws back his head in a huge laugh that goes all the way across to the far side of the lake. Mam is there, sitting on a blanket, and she looks up from her reading, and waves. We both wave back.

The wind picks up a bit, and the water gets choppy, but Da says it's grand for another while. Then I hook something, and it's very heavy and hard to reel in. It takes me a long time. It's drizzling a smur of rain by now, and the boat is really being knocked around in the wind.

When I finally get it to the surface and hook it with the gaff, the rain is so bad I can hardly see. I haul it into the boat. It's so hard to lift it, I have to stand up to get it over the side. It's lying over the side of the boat when I see that it's a body, bloated and rotten, and it's wearing my mam's clothes.

I scream to Da, but his seat is empty. Underneath his seat where the fish were is a pile of big bones.

TWENTY-TWO

I WASN'T DEAD.

I wasn't dead, but if you read the gravestone, I was buried there.

Buried alongside my da. No wonder my mother didn't want to get out of the car that time. The liars must have told her they'd found my body in the lake, and said they'd bury me and my da, or whatever was left of him and his jigsaw-bones, together with me, or whatever was left of me, and get it all over with. I noticed at least they had dumped Uncle Patsy in some other hole at the far side of the graveyard, a good way off from Da. I went looking for his grave, and when I found it, I even said a wee small prayer over it.

'Let's see you kicking the door off your coffin now, you big box of rot,' I said. 'Amen.'

Then I did a wee-wee on the grave. When I was finished, I said, 'Flush that lot, why don't you.'

I went back over to where I was buried with my da.

Well, I escaped from things before, so I knew I'd just have to do it again. Why should it be so hard to escape from a grave? Easy, especially if you're still alive. All you have to do is just dig yourself out.

It was hard work getting Da to escape though. The only good thing was that the ground was still fairly soft. The weather was mild, and there hadn't been much rain since the funeral.

I started digging up my da with my da's own shovel. The very same one he used when he was setting new spuds in the spring. Anyhow, he wasn't really that far down. Maybe because there was no chance of bad smells coming out of the grave, because he was only bones, they just needed a smaller grave. Even so, if he had still been a body, I don't know how I would have got him back up out of the hole. I suppose I was lucky in a way that he was only bones, and it was easy, once I'd broken open a hole in the lid, to get the bones out. I mostly dug up one end of the grave, and broke the coffin lid with the shovel, and a big stone I dropped onto the lid from high up over my head. I nearly did end up buried with Da at one stage, because my arms started to wobble like jelly under the first big rock I lifted, and I thought it was just going to land on my skull. But I got the lid broken open with a smaller rock, and then I was able to sort of slide Da's bones out the broken end. He was all very neatly laid out inside, with his arms down by his side, and his skull on a little pillow, like he was having a nap.

'Ooh, my aching bones,' he used to say.

I pulled the sheet thing out through the hole, like it was a wet sheet off my bed, and most of Da was in that, but not his head, because that was on the pillow on its own. I had to use the flashlamp and crawl a bit into the coffin from the broken end to get his skull. There was no way I was going to go home to my mother without Da's head. What would she say?

'We'll have to say a prayer to Saint Anthony of Padua now that we will find your father's head, JJ. I can't believe the two of you. I shouldn't let the pair of you out together;

you can't be trusted to do the simplest thing. We might as well say the rosary now too.'

And I know what the Sergeant would say too.

'All present and correct,' he would say, when he laid out all my da's bones, his jigsaw finished at last. I noticed too that there was only one coffin there, even though the gravestone said there was two of us in it. I wouldn't be one bit surprised if that miser O'Hanlon who has the funeral undertaker's shop charged my mother for two coffins.

I had a rope tied to the gravestone across from Da's grave, and I used that to scramble back up the side of the hole, where it was steep and slippy. I had to stick some of his small bones in my pockets, or his pockets really, since I was wearing his coat. Then I threw some of the big bones wrapped up in the sheet thing up and out. One of the big long bones, I'm not sure what it was off, got broken in half when I was pulling it out of the coffin. It was at a bad angle, and I think I yanked at it too hard. It was so razor- sharp, I cut my hand on the broken end. I knew Da wouldn't mind that his leg or whatever it was was broken, but then I thought what if a fox or something came along when I was down the hole and took a bone – then what? Enough things had already eaten my da, and I didn't want to have to tell my mother that I had lost anything, or that a part of Da's hip was gone down a badger's hole. So I stopped throwing bones.

I found a fertiliser bag in the ditch, and tied it to a rope around my waist, and put the bones that I already had out of the grave into the bag, and set a big rock on top of it. It was starting to get first light when I had the last of my da in the fertiliser bag and in my pockets, and I was thinking I'd have to leave the grave open till the next night. I couldn't risk filling it back in in daylight, and, anyway, I was just in pure pain after the whole night digging and crawling and pulling bones. Even if the grave was not so deep, it was hard work. I'd never dug up a grave before. It was a quiet graveyard anyhow, and not many people visited it. The ones who used to do the visiting when I was growing up were mostly all dead and buried there themselves by then. So I thought it would be safe enough to leave the grave dug up for one more day. I put all my father's bones in the bag, and got myself ready to finally bring him home to my mother.

I heard a noise behind me. I thought it was a rabbit or something, but when I turned around there was a man standing about three or four feet away from me. I was so busy packing Da away that I'd never noticed or heard anyone coming. Neither of us spoke or moved for a while. He looked over at the pile of earth by the grave, and then back at me. Then I saw he had a shotgun cracked for reloading in the crook of his arm. I wasn't sure if it was intended for rabbits, or for me. After another while, with neither of us saying anything, I thought I'd better explain, even though I mostly knew by then that it was a waste of time ever trying to explain anything to adults.

'I'm not dead at all,' I said.

He just stared at me like I had two heads, which in a way I had, but he said nothing.

'They said I was dead, but I'm not,' I said, and for some reason I started to laugh.

He still said nothing.

I didn't know him. I never remembered ever seeing him anywhere in town or around the fields before.

'My da was hiding, and my mammy was very upset,' I said, trying not to be laughing now. I could see this man thought the whole thing was serious, so I decided it would be better to tell him properly.

'She even put on her awful big hat for weddings and went on the telly. I'm just bringing Da home to her now. It's taken ages, but we'll all be back together again very soon.'

The man didn't move.

I decided to pick up the fertiliser bag of Green Sward Nitrate that Da was in, but then the man moved. He took two cartridges from a pocket in his coat and popped them into the barrels of the shotgun, and cracked the gun shut.

He still didn't say a word, but I could see his face better now that the dawn light was coming up. He looked as shocked as Uncle Patsy did just before he went down with his old jalopy of a van. The man sort of raised the shotgun so it was level with me. I was trying to see if he had the safety catch still on or not, but it wasn't bright enough to get a proper look. I decided that he'd forgotten to take it off, what with him not being sure what to make of me.

'I'll just be off so,' I said, and I went to walk away with the bag of Da. I didn't want to be heading back across the fields in the bright day, and people would be getting up soon.

'Don't,' he said.

'Well, are we just going to stand here all day, staring at each other like two boggle-eyed rabbits with the myxomatosis, or are you going to open your fat gob and spit it out, you bloated gobaloon?'

I knew this was probably not the best way to get on his good side, but I just wanted to make something happen.

'Come on, whoever, or whatever you are. March.' He pointed the two barrels at my head, like I was a prisoner of war. Well, if I was going to be a prisoner of war, then at least we should have a war first, I thought to myself. There I was, about to have my family all back together again, after the upset and terrible times, and now this stranger thought I was going to trot off down to the town and into the police station with my da in a bag of Nitrate 10-10-20! He was wrong. Wrong wrong wrong wrong wrong wrong wrong wrong wrong wrong wrong wrong wrong wrong, and wrong again.

'I can't leave my little brother down in the grave,' I said. 'At least let me get him out of there first. This wasn't even his idea, it was all my fault. I'll even tell that to the Guards.'

He was even more shocked then. He glanced quickly over at the grave as if he was expecting to see a little white hand sticking out and scratching around, searching for something to hold on to and pull itself out of the hole. He edged sideways to the grave, and I sort of edged along with him, carrying Da in front of me. When he got to the side, he looked quickly down at the open hole, and I knew in my heart that was my only chance. I got my hand under the bottom of the fertiliser bag and ran at the man as hard as ever I could with the open end, the end with Da's broken shin bone or whatever it was sticking out.

It was a good shot. Da's leg went into the man sort of where the steering wheel went into Uncle Patsy. Not only that, but the man lost his balance and more or less fell into the hole. The gun didn't go off when he dropped, so I knew I was right about the safety catch still being on. He moved a bit, trying to get out of the hole, and I started to laugh again. We were like a Laurel and Hardy film on television, when one of them got his arse stuck in a barrel. The other one just stood there, scratching his head. The man pulled Da's shin out of him, but I grabbed it and shoved it in again, harder and higher up. Then he got like my mother, with red bubbles in his mouth. It was getting bright, and I knew I didn't have time to ask him if he liked Laurel and Hardy. I lifted his arms inside the hole, and I used the handle of Da's shovel to push his body down into it. I got the rock again, and dropped that in on top of his head too. The noise stopped then, and I was relieved because all the time I was afraid he was going to shout out something stupid – 'Help, it's the murderer boy,' or something like that.

The other good thing was that he nearly filled the hole in for me, so I just dragged a good bit of loose clay over with the shovel from the fresh pile, and filled in whatever was left of the hole after him. Then I had to scoot off mighty fast, because it was nearly bright day, and Dracula needed to get back to the dark cellar. I ended up leaving a bit of Da behind after all. I couldn't pull the shin bone out of the stranger's belly, because of the way he was folded in half down the hole, but I took his loaded shotgun with me instead. Still, it was worth it, I suppose, and I figured I could always go back in a few months and dig that bone out again, if my mother really, really wanted it.

When I got back, I did a quick check to make sure that she was still sulking under her blanket. Her hands were moving away under that blanket, up and down and across and all over the place, like she had more than two hands – ten maybe. She was only looking for attention, and she was stinking for want of a wash, but I didn't go near her or lift up the blanket. I badly needed sleep, and I curled up in the fireplace. The big birthday surprise for my mother would just have to wait. I always knew I'd have to do everything myself, and here at long last was all my family back together again, and just in time to celebrate my twelfth birthday.

TWENTY-THREE

I AM HERE IN THE CASTLE, surrounded by all my family, together again at last, all of us.

Here are the bones, and here are the bones, and here are the bones.

On each side of me.

On each side of me ribs like fingers turning in, curling in to protect.

There's not enough room yet, but soon there will be.

I have to do the crow's work myself. I can't have crows in the tunnel house, making a racket and a mess.

So I need to keep taking out, like the crows did to Da before. Make room for me, like I did in the chimney in the castle.

Make room for myself, keep taking more out.

There will be space for me to lie down there then, with the white rib fingers curling in around to protect me, make me safe again.

I'll lie down in the place where her breast was, where her big heart was, where her belly, that was my first ever castle and hideout, was.

I'll be part of her again, like at the very start. Back then at the very very very very very start.

Then the trouble started, when I left, see? When I left when he left when she left.

Too much leaving, that was all the trouble.

This time not leaving. You can trust bones.

I'm sitting on my da's knee. He is wearing his Sunday best suit, and he is singing a song while he bounces me on his knee. He sang it only for me, and not for anyone else in the world. He said his daddy used to sing it to him too, when he was a wee boy.

It went like this:
There is a happy land far, far away,
Where we get eggs and ham, three times a day,
All the little children run, when they see the butcher come,
There is a happy land far, far away.

My mother is fretting about the place, because she's afraid that we are all going to be late for Mass. She is putting on her good silk headscarf, the one I love, with the horses and bridles and saddles on it. There is a smell of a chicken roasting in the range, and I feel so hungry I want to eat it right now, but we can't because we have to keep our fast before Holy Communion.

Mammy checks the chicken again before we go out to Mass. She pours the grease from the tray over its big golden breast, and it sizzles up and makes my mouth water. Da knows I'm starving, and he's laughing because he knows his song is making me even hungrier.

There is a happy land far, far away,
Where we get hot cross buns, three times a day,
All the little children run, when they see the baker come,
There is a happy land far, far away.

We're nearly ready to go to Mass. Mammy says that the hem on my trousers is falling down on one leg. Da stands me up on a stool and Mam gets her sewing box. She pins back the loose hem and says she'll stitch it later. I like looking at the horses on her headscarf and smelling her soft soapy powdery smell while she's pinning up my loose hem. Da picks a long thread off the back of her coat and blows it softly away.

He gives his hair a quick brush through with the silver-backed brush by the mirror in the hall. Then he lifts me off the stool and sings the rest of his song with me in his arms.

> *There is a happy land far, far away,*
> *Where we get ice-cream cones three times a day,*
> *All the little children run, when they see the ice-man come,*
> *There is a happy land far, far away.*

Mam checks the chicken, and pops in the spuds to roast around it in the range just before we leave. The smell makes my tummy rumble and growl. Da says Mam is like a chicken herself, flapping around the place. Then he holds her hand and gives her a big squelchy kiss on the cheek. Mam goes bright red and says we'll be the last into the church with all his carry-on. Da gives the toe of each shoe a quick shine by rubbing each one in turn on the carpet on the bottom step of the stairs. Mam holds the back door open for us, and as she lets the latch drop, Da starts off again:

There is a happy land far, far away ...

ABOUT GERARD LEE

G erard Lee, a writer, actor and director, graduated with
an M.Phil in Creative Writing from the Oscar Wilde
Centre at Trinity College Dublin in 2007. He has published
poetry in journals such as *Poetry London, An Sionnach*
(Creighton University Press), *Poetry Ireland Review, The Stony
Thursday Book, Southword* and *The SHOp*. He has been a
contributor to *Sunday Miscellany* on RTÉ Radio 1, and is
included in *The Best of Sunday Miscellany 1995–2000*. His work
was also included in *Incorrigibly Plural* (Lemon Soap Press).
He was selected as part of *Poetry Ireland*'s *Introductions* series
in 2007. He has recently completed work on a collection
titled *The Gift of Nails*.

His play on a meeting between Sir William Wilde and
James Clarence Mangan, *Mangan's Last Gasp*, was performed
to critical acclaim in Bewley's Café Theatre in 2013, and
another play *A New Day* was presented at the same venue
in May 2014.

Gerard originally trained as an actor at the Samuel
Beckett Centre in Trinity College Dublin. Theatre
performances include *The Flaying of Marsyas* by Joe O'Byrne

(Flat Lake Festival), *Operation Easter* by Donal O'Kelly for Calypso Theatre Company, *Behind the Green Curtain* for O'Casey Theatre Co., *Uncle Vanya* for Field Day (Gate), *Woyzeck, The Sinking of the Titanic, Tales from the Vienna Woods, Cabaret/Kabarett* (with Agnes Bernelle) and *Departed,* all for Co-Motion, *Hades* and *Epic* with Upstate. He appeared in *The Poor Mouth* at the Edinburgh Theatre Festival, where the show won the *Guardian* Critic's Award. He also appeared in *Berlin Alexanderplatz* at the Edinburgh Festival, where he played Franz Biberkopf. Other theatre work includes *The Billy Club Puppets* for Peter Sheridan and *The Salvage Shop* (Garter Lane) for Jim Nolan.

Television and film acting credits include *Father Ted, Mattie, Kilinaskully, Fair City, Proof 2, Glenroe, Vicious Circle, Rough Diamond, Ordinary Decent Criminal* and *Angela's Ashes.*

Gerard worked for a number of years in residential care, with young people living apart from their families. He has been active in developing youth arts with socially marginalised young people.